# PARACHUTE

HOLLY RAE GARCIA

"... Out of SPACE - out of TIME.
   Bottomless vales and boundless floods,
   And chasms, and caves and Titan woods,
   With forms that no man can discover
   For the tears that drip all over..."

— "DREAM-LAND" BY EDGAR ALLAN POE

*Dedicated to B'wood, Class of '97*

# 1

It was one of those rare summer nights where the breeze blowing in off the coast provided a small break from the suffocating heat. Angela Rodriguez was running late to meet her friends, *again*. She couldn't remember a time when she wasn't late for something. Her Dad liked to say, "If you're early, you're on time. If you're on time, you're late." He was more than slightly disappointed she hadn't inherited that gene.

Angela bounded down their maroon-carpeted stairs, skipping every other one before grabbing the end of the banister and swinging herself over the last two steps and around into their living room. Not that her family ever did much "living" in that room, except to play Nintendo or watch Wheel of Fortune. Along one wall was a seldom-used, large brick fireplace, aesthetically pleasing more than anything else. They probably lit it around five times in the winter when a cold front blew down from the North. Built up from the floor about a foot, the base consisted of tan and white bricks, and those same bricks continued up to the ceiling. On either side of the fireplace mantle were two long-dead things: a large, white-tail deer head that had hung there for as long as Angela could remember, and the other, a dust-covered boar head. A stuffed bobcat glued to a dead log sat on the raised edge of the fireplace. Angela hated that thing. If she wasn't careful, the sharp ends of the branches would grab her legs when she walked by. The small rubber tongue was removable, loosened by prying fingers over the years. Her dad liked to take it out and place it in odd spots around the house, hoping to scare her and her mom.

Angela headed for the kitchen, looking for her parents. They were probably seated around the large island or at the high bar facing the dining room table. "The kitchen is the heart of the home," said someone some time ago. Probably her grandma.

Her mom was there, pulling dinner out of the oven. Another *casserole*. Angela frowned. A casserole was not at all what she expected from the mouth-watering smells. Ever since her mom started the jazzercise class down at Skating America, she kept trying out recipes from the other ladies in attendance. Before that, she had never even *eaten* a casserole, much less cooked one. Her mom set the heavy dish on a braided potholder on the counter with a thud and pulled the oven mitts from her hands. Her thick, curly hair was pulled back into a bun, but a few strands had escaped. She pushed them off her tan forehead with the back of her hand and smiled at Angela.

Angela couldn't have timed it any better if she had tried. Casseroles were just mush layered with mush, and no texture. Sometimes her mom would throw a handful of crushed Dorito chips on top. Then it was *almost* palatable.

Her dad stood in front of the large island at the center of the kitchen, chopping tomatoes and cucumbers for a salad. He could be a meticulous man and took great care to make sure everything was evenly chopped. Angela had told him a million times that no one cared, as long as it tasted good.

Angela tugged a scrunchie from her wrist and pulled her own curly, brown hair into a high ponytail. She grabbed her keys from a hook on the wall and lifted her overnight bag off a bar stool.

"I'm heading to Val's, see y'all mañana."

"Are you sure you don't wanna eat first? It'll be cool enough in a few minutes."

"No, ma'am. We're doing pizza."

"Okay. Tell her I said hello. And don't do anything stupid that'll get you killed. You know there's a serial killer off 45." Her mother shook her finger at Angela.

She sighed. "Mom, take a chill pill. That's like, almost an *hour* away and I'm not going anywhere near there."

"¡N'ombre! Alex, do you hear my own daughter talking to me like this?"

Her dad looked up from the cutting board. "Angela Marie, don't sass your mother. Just promise her you won't go near 45."

Angela shifted her weight to her other leg, impatient. "Didn't that stuff stop like, years ago?"

Her mom wagged her finger in the air and said, "You know they never caught him. He could still be out there."

"Fine, I promise." She looked at her dad for help, some backup that her mom was once again being overly protective. A retired serial killer off a highway an hour away was not her primary concern.

Her dad kept chopping tomatoes and muttered, "Be careful driving," without lifting his eyes from the cutting board.

"Yes, sir."

Angela didn't roll her eyes until she cleared the front

door. Always the same thing. Say hello to friends (she never did), avoid serial killers (like, *duh*), and be careful driving (she always was). She pulled her shorts back down beneath her hips, leaving a few inches of bare skin visible beneath her white crocheted top, and unlocked her car.

## 2

Angela's gray 1984 Mercury Cougar limped down the highway like a dying elephant. She used to refer to it as "The Boat," but her best friend Valerie Linscomb had once called it "The Silver Bullet" as a joke and the name stuck. It wasn't pretty, but it got her from point A to point B and that was really all she needed. Well, she could do without the air conditioner that leaked ice-cold water on her feet every time she took a sharp left turn. Her grandpa had shown her how to unclog the line with a coat hanger, but she always forgot until it was too late, and her feet were soaked in freezing water.

Val lived about fifteen minutes away, on the other side of the Intracoastal canal. She and her twin brother, Shawn, had lived with their grandpa in his beach house ever since their parents died in a car wreck when they were only eight years old. Shawn and Val had been sleeping in the backseat when it happened. Some idiot had rammed their car into the side railing at the top of the Intracoastal canal bridge, just past the crest. By the time her parents came over the bridge and saw the car, they were going too fast to stop.

They clipped the back end of the other vehicle, sending it flying over the concrete barrier and into the waters below. Their car flipped but, thankfully, had landed in the other lane of the bridge. Cars coming up that side were able to see the wreck in time to slow down. The twins had no recollection of what happened. Just that they were asleep one minute, and the next they were watching their parents' blood pool onto the roof of their car as they all hung upside down from their seatbelts.

Their grandpa had stepped up and taken the twins in, and that's where they lived ever since. He was a kind old man, but the years were taking their toll on him physically. Mentally, he could be as spry as a sixteen-year-old. Just the weekend before, he had stayed with his younger-by-two-decades girlfriend over in Beaumont. Said they spent the entire weekend naked. That's about when Val and Shawn shooed Angela out of their house, embarrassed.

The beach house wasn't a whole lot to look at. Years of wind-whipped sand and sun had taken their toll. The once bright blue wooden planks had seen better days, and a few hung at odd angles. The air conditioner, propped high up on a platform on the side of the house, dripped condensation down onto the same spot it had for years, leaving a small rust-stained pool on the concrete below. Back when it was brand new, they had enjoyed an uninterrupted view of the Gulf of Mexico. Over the years, big investors from out of town had built huge, multi-family-sized beach houses and rented them out for reunions and other big parties. The larger houses blocked the view of the water, but they could still be on the beach via a two-minute walk, so it wasn't so bad.

Angela eased the Silver Bullet onto the sandy patch of sparse grass in front of the house, in between Jason Crawford's old brown and black Chevy Chevette and Eric Hernandez's orange Ford Pinto. Both cars had "Class of '97" scrawled on every window in white acrylic paint. Angela had removed the same sentiments from her own car just the day before.

When she opened her car door, a gust of salty wind whipped her ponytail and a seagull cawed above her. She glanced at the front seat of Jason's Chevy as she walked past, spotting her boyfriend Doug Jackson's backpack sitting on the passenger seat. They must have ridden together.

The boys told their parents they were having a sleepover at Shawn's house, and the girls told their parents they were having a sleepover at Val's. Which technically wasn't a lie. They did plan to eventually go back to the beach house. But none of the parents knew their grandpa had gone out of town, riding his Harley on his annual trek to Sturgis. And they were definitely not aware of the fact that boys and girls would be staying over at the same time.

Angela and her friends had all graduated from Brazoswood High School the day before, though Jason and Eric skipped the chance to walk with their class so they could get a head start on packing. Those two never did care much for pomp and circumstance. They would head straight for Austin in three weeks, where they were going to rent an apartment and look for summer jobs before the Fall semester started at the University of Texas. Everyone, including Angela, had told them it was too late, that there wouldn't be any summer jobs left in a college town like that, but they didn't listen. Or just didn't care. Either way, they were getting the hell out of that small town.

Angela had decided college wasn't really for her. She wanted to *live* a little first. She had no idea what she wanted to do for the rest of her life and didn't want to waste her parent's money changing majors every semester like she knew she would. What seventeen-year-old had any clue what they wanted to do for a living? She sure as hell didn't. Angela liked to figure things out as she went, never was one for planning. That didn't make for much of an answer when everyone over the age of forty would ask, "So, what are your plans after high school?" The fuck if she knew, and that's how she liked it.

# 3

---

The ocean roared behind her as Angela trudged up the steps to the front door. The old wood groaned while she climbed upward, her hand carefully touching the splintering railing as she went. At the top, a wrap-around porch encircled the entire house, but everyone knew not to go around back. The wood there had rotted, and it was a quick trip to busting her ass through the floor and straight down if she dared step onto the old boards. Angela placed her hand on the doorknob and stopped, peering through the scratched glass at the center of the door.

Val lounged sideways on an old plaid recliner in the living room, playing with her pager. Her short, pale legs draped lazily over one of the armrests. She wore her favorite outfit that no amount of pleading from Angela could convince her to put away: denim short overalls, one side unsnapped and hanging down, over a hot pink tank top with black straps. Her straight, blonde hair hung in a bob at her shoulders, held in place by a black headband that matched a velvet choker around her neck. Curled bangs dusted her small forehead.

Val had a full ride to Baylor for softball but wasn't leaving for a few months yet since her dorm wouldn't be ready until early August. Her older-by-five-minutes twin brother Shawn planned to hang around town and go to Brazosport Community College over in Clute for a year or two, then said he would probably transfer to a four-year university. *As if*. Shawn was a great dude— kind, thoughtful, and he would give anyone the shirt off his back. But Shawn Linscomb stayed perpetually high. He drifted through life with a smile on his face and a doobie in his pocket.

At that moment, he sat slouched on a matching plaid couch, a video game remote in his hand with a thin black cord leading to the tv in front of him. He wore black ripped jeans that were almost as wide at his ankles as they were at his thighs and a black Nirvana t-shirt. He wouldn't be caught dead in shorts, even in the summertime. Shawn had one note in his wardrobe, and that note was black. The only thing that wasn't black was the silver wallet chain hanging from his waist that disappeared into his pocket. He even tried to dye his shaggy blond hair black one summer, but it came out green, so he had gone bald for the rest of the year as if he meant to do it. His black combat boots (from Col. Bubbie's, the Army surplus store in Galveston) were propped up on the coffee table, laces untied, as Shawn played *Legend of Zelda*. It happened to be one of Angela's favorite games, though she wasn't as good as Shawn yet. Her parents had finally decided to leave the ice age and upgrade their Atari for a Nintendo, and she'd only had the game a few months.

Jason sat next to Shawn, staring at the TV. Jason changed his style like most people changed their underwear, but that week he wore an unbuttoned flannel shirt over a white Green Day T-shirt and jeans, with old Skechers.

Off to the right was a small round table with four wooden chairs. Behind the table, a kitchen had been shoved into the small space like a fat guy in a little coat. Chipped yellow tiles clung to the counter and ran halfway up the walls. Kitchen utensils and plates overflowed onto a card table pressed into the corner.

In the kitchen, Eric and Doug were busy digging into a cardboard box on the counter, slapping greasy slices of pepperoni and cheese pizza onto paper towels. Eric wiped one hand on his Pearl Jam T-shirt and pulled his long denim shorts up with the other hand. He flipped his head to get his stringy, brown hair out of his eyes and saw Angela through the glass door. Eric nodded his head at her as he dug into a slice of pepperoni pizza. She forced a smile, then turned her attention back to the living room.

Jason pulled away from watching the video game and looked toward the door. His eyes widened and he immediately fought down his quick smile, resulting in an awkward grimace. Jason glanced behind him at the kitchen before wiping his palm across his forehead and returning to the TV.

Angela took a deep breath and pushed the door open. Might as well get the night over with. It wasn't her idea, them all hanging out together like this, but Val had insisted and kept reminding them it might be one of the last times they could do it before everyone scattered toward uncertain futures.

"Hey!" Doug wiped his hands on his pants, leaving pizza-grease smears across the light acid-washed jeans, and walked over to her. Smiling, he grabbed her waist and pulled her close to him. His hands were cold against her bare stomach. "It's about time you got here."

He pressed his lips against hers, his tongue trying to explore more, but she pulled away.

"You okay?"

"Yeah, I'm good," said Angela, walking past him toward the kitchen. "Just hungry, did y'all save me any?"

"Of course, here you go babe." Doug handed her his plate with what were apparently the last two pieces of pizza.

"Thanks a lot," Angela mumbled.

"My bad."

At least Doug managed to look sheepish, though she could never tell since any hint of a blush lay hidden beneath his dark brown skin.

"I thought maybe you ate before you came."

"Hey! What took you so long?" Val swung her legs down to the floor and stood up, stretching.

"Had to chat with the parental units, you know how they are."

"Well, let's bounce!" Val walked in front of Shawn, blocking his view of the video game. He tilted to the side to try to see around her, but she grabbed the cord dangling between the TV and the remote and yanked, pulling it loose.

"Hey!" Shawn scrambled to plug the cord back in before a one-eyed hopping crab could kill Link, but it was too late. The character spun in a circle and the screen turned red, then black, as he died.

"You don't have to be such a bitch." He glared at his sister.

Val huffed, "You suck anyway."

"Hey Shawn, got any batteries? My pager is dead, and my mom will, like, *murder* me if she can't reach me. She's such a fucking stalker," Eddie said.

Angela said, "My mom likes to say she wants to know

where I am so she'd know where to start looking for my body if I was killed."

"God, your mom is so fucking morbid." Val laughed.

Angela shrugged, not much she could say to counter that. Her mom *was* morbid.

Val grabbed her keys from a hook by the front door and turned to Angela, "You didn't tell your mom our grandpa was out of town, did you?"

"*As if*, what do you think I am, an idiot?" Angela asked.

"Well, you are dating *him*." Val smiled and tilted her head toward Doug.

"Can't argue there, I don't know what she sees in me, either," said Doug, laughing.

"I'm going to the bathroom. Then we're ready, yeah?" called Angela, over her shoulder as she walked down the short hallway.

"Yeah, meet y'all downstairs. Lock the door behind you," said Val, as she opened the front door and she and Doug followed the others down the stairs.

When Angela emerged from the restroom, she realized Jason had stayed behind.

"Hey," he whispered, smiling shyly.

"Hey," Angela answered, looking past him through the glass door. Everyone else had already gone down the stairs.

They were alone.

He took a step toward her and reached out to grab her hand.

"Not here, Jason. *Jesus*."

Angela walked past him, grabbed the two slices of pizza, and stepped halfway through the door before she turned to look at him. The wounded look on his face faded as they stared at each other. She turned away before anything else could happen.

"Lock the door behind you."

Angela bounded down the stairs, taking them two at a time.

They all piled into the only vehicle large enough for everyone, the Blue Ford Econoline Van that Shawn and Val shared. She had saved the front passenger seat for Angela. Val stepped on the gas a little too hard, and the back tires flung sand up behind them as they peeled out of the driveway and headed toward town. Angela glanced at the boys in the back seat. Her boyfriend grinned and winked and, behind him in the very last row of seats, Jason smiled.

Angela sighed and turned back around to face the road, a large rip in the leather seat scratching her thigh. She should have worn longer shorts, she always seemed to forget how uncomfortable Val's front seat could be. She took a bite of lukewarm pizza.

"You good, chica?" Val asked, keeping her eyes and both hands on the wheel as they went over the bridge back to the mainland. Her knuckles tightened. Angela knew Val didn't need to remember the crash to be haunted by it; that bridge was full of her ghosts.

"Yeah, all good."

"Good, because we are going to parrrtyyy," said Val, before taking a deep breath and forcing a laugh as they pulled off the bridge. She shifted to one side and dug into her pocket, balancing the steering wheel with one hand.

"Oh, no."

"Oh, *yes!*" Val chuckled as she waved a joint in the air between them, "and Eric has more."

"Of *course,* Eric has more." Angela smiled.

"Can y'all quit fucking around and turn up the music?" Eric called from the backseat.

They cruised down Highway 332, singing along loudly,

and quite badly, to "Pepper" by the Butthole Surfers. Angela propped her feet on the dashboard, remembering (and ignoring) her mother's warning. 'Don't put your feet there, if you get in a wreck, it'll drive your legs straight into your chest and your knees will break your skull open.' Not that she knew a single person that had ever happened to, but it didn't stop her mom from voicing the dire warnings.

# 4

Val slowed the van as they turned onto North Mahan Street. They drove past the Richwood Community Center on their right, a small tin building where Angela's Girl Scout troop had hosted a sleepover, back when her mom could still make her join things like the Girl Scouts. Technically, it was the Brownies. Like, a *Junior* Girl Scout. She convinced her mom to let her quit before she graduated to full-fledged Scout. Of course, Angela had waited until after that sleepover where a hunk of fudge the size of a toddler had been promised *and* delivered. She had a stomachache for two days afterward. It had been, like, *totally* worth it. After that, the last time she had been in the Community Center was for her Aunt Inez's baby shower last April. It was seriously the lamest place to have any event and she had no idea why anyone would even want to be there. Out of the two window-unit air-conditioners, only one worked consistently. The ancient phone was one of those rotary things that took forever to dial, and the chipboard walls were peppered with holes.

Angela and her friends were lucky that night, all the

lights were off and the parking lot sat empty. Events meant cops. Well, the good events, anyway. The ones with alcohol. And cops meant a hitch in their plans.

The road veered to the right and Val shoved her foot onto the gas, giving everyone whiplash as she swung the van around the sharp curve.

"Jesus, Val!" complained Jason, as he rubbed the side of his head. "You knocked me into the glass."

"Don't be such a bitch," Val laughed.

Angela turned to look out the window as they pulled into the parking lot of Polk Elementary school, where Angela had attended Kindergarten through fifth grade. The lot was empty, as expected, and they headed around back toward the old playground. Even if it wasn't summer, no one would have been there. The school had been abandoned ever since it flooded back in '95. Not from the usual hurricane or tropical storm flooding, but heavy rains north of Houston had dumped too much water into the Brazos River. The river couldn't be contained by the banks on its southward trek toward the Gulf of Mexico, spilling out and flooding a few homes, businesses, and one elementary school. Rumor had it that everything would have been fine, but one of the higher-end towns nearby had diverted the pumps so their town wouldn't have any flooding. The political fallout afterward had been intense, and Angela still didn't understand what all happened, just that the fancy town didn't see a drop of water, and this one had flooded. The damage was irreparable, and the school had closed for good. Most of the furniture and supplies remained behind, water-logged and molding. The school had donated the playground equipment to the local Boys and Girls Club. Only the support poles remained, jutting out from the ground at odd angles.

Two blue dumpsters sat next to each other in front of about fifty acres of woods that had somehow remained untouched by the recent developers. Most of the people in the town were quite all right with that since rumor had it the forest was haunted. More than a few people had gone back there and never returned. They joked that it was the Bermuda Triangle of South-East Texas, or that it contained an old Indian burial ground. Because of course it would. Ever since they saw Poltergeist, Jason and Eric blamed everything on someone's ancient burial ground. No one really knew the history of the woods and Angela had never explored it. The whole thing creeped her out a little too much. Besides, she had personally known one of the missing people. Two, actually. Her old babysitter Carol had gone in there with her boyfriend Todd back in the summer of '84 and hadn't been seen since. Angela had met the boyfriend a few times when Carol snuck him into the house after Angela was supposed to be asleep. Carol knew she wasn't allowed to have friends over, especially *boys*, when she babysat. But, since Angela had grown up and discovered sex herself, she completely understood and would have snuck Jason in anywhere she could have gotten away with it. *Doug.* She meant Doug, of course. Doug, her boyfriend.

Angela's mom, a fervent disbeliever in all things spiritual or strange, blamed Carol's boyfriend. Said he probably chopped Carol up into little pieces and took off for Nevada. For some reason, she always assumed people fled to Nevada even though the Mexican border was *right there* and a much more logical place if one were looking to flee the long arm of the law. Her mom also said wild animals probably ate the broken, chopped up remains of Carol, and that's why no one ever found a trace of her. Angela's mom liked to think she had an answer for everything. An incredibly dark and morbid answer, but an answer, nonetheless.

The van's tires ground along the broken pavement before rolling to a stop in front of the old gymnasium. There were gaps and cracks throughout the white-painted bricks. Even when the school had been filled with kids, the gym was a piece of crap. It was built before anything else on the school grounds. Back in the twenties, some weird church owned the property and they used the building for all of their big events, weddings, bake-offs, or whatever churches did with shit like that. The main building, the one they held their services in, sat about forty feet away. It had been turned into a library when the school was built. Rows of books covered the walls, with more books on shelves in-between. It had been a great library. The only things left that still resembled the old church were the red stained-glass windows facing the woods. Someone important enough must have thought it was a good piece of history or had character or something. Angela just thought they just looked creepy. Who installed *red* stained-glass windows, anyway? Bloody shafts of light didn't exactly scream, "let's get all churchy up in here."

Angela slid the van door open and stepped out onto the pavement. The final sounds of Nirvana's "Heart-Shaped Box" cut off abruptly as Val pulled the key from the ignition. The headlights cut out, leaving only the soft glow from a full moon in a cloudless sky. The night was quiet, and the sounds of shoes crunching on asphalt, and doors closing shut with a thud, seemed to echo around them.

Doug climbed onto the hood of Val's van and carefully shuffled to the end. He stepped onto a ledge with one foot, held tight to the framework of the building, and shifted himself upward. The momentum brought his hands to the edge of the roof, and he pulled himself up and over it with a grunt. Eric was next, clearing it faster than Doug had. Shawn helped Val up, then went behind her. Jason put his hands on Angela's waist to help guide her, but she pushed him off.

"I got it," she huffed as she climbed, keenly aware of the brooding silence behind her.

By the time Jason climbed onto the roof, Angela was halfway across, heading toward the others and their favorite spot at the far end, closest to the woods. Tucked away enough that anyone passing wouldn't see their flashlights or lit ends of their joints, they still had a great view of the woods and the peaceful near silence throughout.

Shawn and Val had already cleared a section of most of the dirt and leaves and were sitting down, their backs leaning against the short ledge at the edge of the roof. Eric stood in front of them, pulling a small plastic bag from his pocket. He opened it with a flourish and grinned.

"I got the goods. Who's in?"

"I'm *definitely* in," said Jason, smiling.

"I got my own shit," Val mumbled around the tip of the roach in her mouth as she tried to light it.

They didn't bother asking Angela if she wanted any, or acting surprised when she didn't join in. She never did, wasn't the type to like any sort of loss of control. Hell, she wouldn't even be a part of their group if it weren't for Doug. She had known who they all were, since their town was so damn small, but would never have hung out with any of them. Not even Haley, who had since become her very best friend. They joked that she was uptight, and maybe they were right. She knew she could probably stand to relax a little, but tonight wasn't the night for it. She needed to stay on top of Jason's current mood. He seemed to be wanting to put everything out in the open, or at least tease at it. She would have to do something quickly. The whole "love triangle" was harshing the vibe of their hangouts lately.

Doug lowered himself to a sitting position next to Angela and reached for her hand. She didn't pull away. He smiled and leaned over to kiss her. He wasn't a bad guy. There wasn't anything at all wrong with him. Smart and funny, he could be goofy in that sweet way that she couldn't help but love. And he loved her more than anyone ever had. Fiercely and selflessly.

They were each other's first *everything*. Angela and Doug had been inseparable since they started dating their freshman year. They were great together. She didn't know what was wrong with her, that she had done those things with Jason. And worse, had enjoyed it. Wanted to do it again. She hated herself for it but couldn't stop.

She needed to end things with Doug, needed to let him go to UCLA without the pressure of maintaining a long-distance relationship with her. He deserved better than the shit she was doing to him.

# 5

The night sky stretched out above them, and the full moon caressed everything with a light glow. Crickets sang in the grass, their lullaby had put Angela to sleep all her life. At home, her bedroom was on the second floor and her window overlooked a slough in their backyard. Crickets and bullfrogs were a nightly concert for her. When the moon was full, like now, she could usually see the Nutria Rats outlined against the water, sitting on the banks. She loved to watch them from her window.

Doug dropped her hand as they moved to lay down on their backs next to each other. Once settled, he grabbed it again and squeezed as if he were afraid to let go. Afraid to let *her* go.

Angela kept her eyes on the stars and whispered, "Isn't it so peaceful?"

He leaned over and kissed her on the cheek, then settled in closer to her. Doug's body felt warm, soft, and familiar. He smelled clean and soapy, of Calvin Klein cologne and Herbal Essences Shampoo.

Smoke drifted over from where the others chilled in

silence. Val had moved over to an old cooling unit across from Eric and Shawn and sat with her legs crossed in front of her, her head tilted back, and eyes closed. She pulled her hand up to her face and breathed in, then a puff of smoke engulfed her. Shawn sat with his legs out in front of him and Eric's head resting comfortably in his lap in that familiar way of two people who really *knew* each other. Shawn ran his fingers through Eric's brown hair absent-mindedly as he smoked. The two had been on-again-off-again since sophomore year and didn't look like they were any closer to figuring out what they wanted from each other, much less what they wanted to do for the rest of their lives. Angela didn't know a single person who *did* know what they wanted out of life. Even the adults didn't seem to have it together.

Jason lay near them on his back with his hands behind his head, also staring up at the stars. He leaned up on one elbow with a grunt and reached a hand toward Val.

"Hey, save me some."

He took the joint from her and settled back down, smoking as he returned his eyes to the stars.

Everyone breathed in the night. No parents yelling at them or homework overdue. No one expecting them to know what to do after high school. No bullshit. Just each other and the darkness. Angela sighed. She loved those nights on the roof but knew they would soon be coming to an end.

"It's all just bullshit, you know?" Eric whispered after exhaling smoke and lifting his hand to pass the joint to Shawn above him.

"What's bullshit?" Jason called out.

"*Everything.* College. Life. Capitalism. We're all just killing ourselves, and for what? Nothing, man. Fucking *nothing.* I hate this fucking town, and all its dead ends and small-minded people."

"Yeah, man," Shawn agreed.

Angela smiled. She was going to miss Eric waxing philosophical as he got high.

"I don't know, doesn't seem that complicated," said Doug, squeezing Angela's hand again. "Graduate high school, check. Go to college... *soon.* Graduate again, get those jobs, make the *good* money. Not have to worry about the small shit anymore."

"Yeah, but that's just it, man. It's *all* small shit. And why do you have to go to college? It's such a scam. They tell us what to do, where to be." Eric's voice drifted off and his eyes fluttered closed.

Val said, "What's a Saturday night without 'Deep Thoughts from Eric Hernandez'?"

The others chuckled while Eric kept his eyes closed. Weed always relaxed him a little *too* much.

"You know, I went to this elementary school," Angela said, turning her head to face her friends.

"We *know*, you mention it every time we come up here," Val laughed.

Angela was the only one in the group who had gone to Polk. The others attended Madge Griffith on the other side of town, and Jason, well Jason went to Elementary school somewhere up in New York. He didn't move to Texas until ninth grade. Angela remembered when he first showed up in Mrs. Abernathy's Home Ec. Class. He sauntered in, seemingly not at all afraid of a new school or trying to make new friends. Jason was an Army brat and had never really stayed anywhere longer than a year or two. That year, his stepdad had finished his last tour and was discharged from the Army, so they had decided to settle on the Texas Coast.

Every girl at Brazoswood High School had a crush on the new guy with the Yankee accent. Even his *hair* had seemed cooler than the other guys. The "new" eventually wore off, and the girls moved on. Most of them, anyway.

Angela turned back toward the night sky. "Well, I *did*. Man, I used to love gym class. Remember those big sticks that, like, one person on each end held them and they moved them apart and together and you, like, jumped through them? What were those called?"

"Fuck if I know, click-clack sticks? Kanicky sticks? Click-aty? Something that sounds like that," Val answered as she smoked, small puffs of air drifting from her mouth. "Those *were* fun, until the holders decided to be assholes and catch your ankle in 'em.

"I liked the parachute," Doug chimed in.

"What the fuck are you talking about?" asked Jason, as he smiled lazily.

"You know, that big fabric thing everyone flung up in the air while you held on to the edge and ran under it and held it down and sat on it so it, like, ballooned up above you and you were all inside together?" Doug explained.

"Oh yeah," Angela said.

"Oh, I remember that!" Val grinned.

"I think I remember," said Shawn, reluctantly, "but we threw, like, balls on it and bounced them around. Your way sounds a lot more fun."

Jason whispered, "You know what we should do... because I have no fucking idea what y'all are talking about. Must be a redneck Texas thing. Anyway, we should go see if they still have one down there. Then y'all can show me what the fuck this thing is, 'cause all I'm picturing is a fucking parachute like, to jump out of a plane with. And that makes *no* sense."

"You know, that's not a bad idea!" Val jumped to her feet.

"Oh no," Angela said. "Let's just stay here and chill. I'm not in the mood for breaking and entering. They probably cleared everything out, anyway."

"Let's do it!" Doug stood up, pulling Angela by the hand to stand next to him. He pulled a little too hard and she fell into him, laughing.

Angela steadied, then brushed the dust off the bottom of her shorts and smiled at Doug.

"Ok, so let's do it," said Val, as she ground out the embers of the joint onto the rooftop before shoving the roach back in her pocket.

"Fine," Angela answered.

Shawn jostled a now-sleeping Eric awake. "Hey, we're gonna go down inside the gym, see something 'bout a parachute."

"Sure man, sure," Eric mumbled as he stood up and stretched his arms. He looked around for the joint they were sharing then eyed Shawn. "Man, you didn't save me any?"

Shawn laughed, "You had practically the whole thing, dude."

Eric stared at him from beneath heavy-lidded eyes and yawned.

"It's okay, let's just go down," said Shawn, as he took Eric by the hand and they walked back to the edge of the roof where they had climbed up.

The trip down was much faster than the one going up, and soon everyone stood next to the van.

"So how do we do this thing?" asked Angela, hoping she sounded braver than she felt.

"There's a window over here, looks like we could break it," Shawn piped up.

"No," Angela argued. She drew the line at the destruction of property.

"Look, the place is already condemned, right? What are they gonna do? Replace the fucking window?" Shawn said.

"He's right," Doug said, "no one's gonna give a shit."

Before Angela could argue any further, Jason picked up a large rock from the edge of the parking lot and walked toward them.

"This should do it."

He pulled his arm back and threw the rock as hard as he could at the old glass window. It shattered easily, and when the final tinkle of glass hitting the pavement stopped, the woods behind them were silent. No crickets, no frogs. *Nothing*. Angela and her friends froze, waiting for sirens or someone to come tell them they weren't supposed to be there, and definitely weren't supposed to be breaking into a school, but no one came.

"Well, I guess we're doing this," mumbled Eric, still half asleep.

Jason found another rock and used it to break away the sharp edges from the window frame, tossing it inside next to the other one.

Doug, the most athletic of the group, intertwined his fingers and turned his hands palms up before saying, "Who's first?"

He knelt and Val placed one foot in the cup of his hands, one hand on his shoulder, and the other against the building.

"On the count of three," Doug said. "One, two, *three*." He grunted as he lifted her up to the windowsill.

"Damnit, Jason, you didn't get all the edges." Val held her hands up to show the group the blood seeping from the fine cuts along her palms.

"You're okay – who's next?"

One by one they were hoisted through the window by Doug until only he and Angela were left standing alone outside the gymnasium. He looked around and spotted a large cinder block. Running over to grab it, he returned and placed it beneath the window.

"Should have done this sooner, could have saved my hands some work," he laughed.

Angela smiled, stepped onto the block, and pulled herself up through the window. Doug assisted by way of his hands on her ass, and when she glanced back with an eyebrow raised, he shrugged and said, "Hey, just helping out," as he winked at her.

Once Angela was inside, Doug climbed onto the block and followed her through the broken window.

His feet landed with a crunchy thud on the glass-spattered, wooden gymnasium floor, the sound echoing off the empty walls.

# 6

The gym was almost pitch-black, with only a slight glow coming through the windows from the full moon outside. They stayed in the middle of the room, whispering to each other as their eyes adjusted to the dim interior.

Doug grabbed Angela's hand and leaned in close. She thought he might try to kiss her, but he shifted his head toward her ear and whispered, "Hey, can we talk?"

She nodded, then realizing he may not have been able to see her, whispered back, "Sure."

Doug led Angela into a corner of the gymnasium next to a stack of retractable bleachers. The wooden seats were water-swollen a few feet up the stack and had white patches of mold growing on them.

"Not sure this is a good spot to be breathing the air," said Angela, eyeing the mold.

Doug reached out and grabbed her hands. "Hey, are we good?"

"Huh?" Angela kept her eyes on the mold.

"Are we *good*? You've been... weird lately."

Angela sighed and looked at him. Large, brown eyes stared back at her. "Sure, we're good." She searched his face for any knowledge of a reason things *wouldn't* be good between them.

Doug smiled and pulled her against him. They kissed in the darkness, by the mold-covered bleachers. Angela figured it was a decent metaphor for their relationship. A relationship she didn't know how to end, or even if she wanted it to end. She loved Doug, she was pretty sure. But she also felt *alive* with Jason. And she knew it was wrong, they both did. They never meant for any of it to happen.

They had all been night fishing over at Val and Shawn's a few months before, and it was her turn to swim the bait out past the second sandbar. She was terrified of swimming in the ocean at night, the way she could feel the waves licking her body but couldn't see them. The water was just a vast nothing with the occasional glint of a reflected moon on a passing wave. She couldn't see the things brushing against her as they swam close. Semi-dried seaweed floating on the top of the water felt like a shark's rough skin, and shells kicked by toes could be a crab about to pinch. Doug usually walked out with her, but he was the one with the pole, so Jason volunteered to help. She had thought nothing of it at first, even though she had noticed the way he'd been looking at her lately. How was she to know, that when they were past the first sandbar and out of sight of the others on that moonless night, an electric shock would consume her when he grabbed her waist? When he pulled her in and kissed her, his hands exploring her body like she had never been touched before. Red-hot fire seemed to come from his fingertips. It took her breath away, she had never felt anything like that before, and certainly not with Doug. She surprised herself, and Jason, when she kissed him back.

And even more later, when they made it to the second sandbar and could touch the bottom, when she put her hand down his swim trunks and grabbed him, guiding him into her as their feet dug into the sand. She had chalked the impulsivity up to a bad fight with Doug that morning, and way too many beers that night.

No one could see them. The only witness to their act was a school of shocked mullet jumping out of the water a few feet away, and it was over quickly. They had rushed to finish dropping the line and head back, breathless from what the others could assume was just a rough swim against a strong tide.

They had met secretly and had sex countless times since then. Of course, she was still sleeping with Doug, too. She didn't want him to think anything was wrong. And he didn't seem to suspect anything, not in those months of secrecy, and not at that moment standing in the dark gym as he looked into her eyes.

"Oh my god, guys. Come look over here," Jason shouted.

They broke eye contact and emerged from the corner. The rest of the group stood in front of a door that must have been open when the floodwaters hit. The swollen, rotting wood hung from one hinge at an odd angle. In better days, it had enclosed a storage room for gym equipment and junk.

Jason pulled a box from the shadows. The crumbling bottom of the cardboard broke apart as it rubbed against the floor, spilling the contents.

"Ugh, y'all had these too?" Jason laughed as he pulled gray shirts from a pile on the floor. Every other one had holes in the armpits, and all of them were stained yellowish from years of pre-pubescent sweat. "Man, I hated wearing these, no matter how many times you took them home to wash, they always smelled like Shawn's ass."

Shawn punched Jason on his arm. "You wish you knew what my ass smelled like."

"I think Eric is the only one who should know what Shawn's ass smells like," Val said.

Eric laughed, "I love you dude, but I'm pleading the fifth on that one."

Shawn smiled, "Whatever, man."

"What's that?" asked Val, pointing to a large mass sitting on top of a pile of boxes further back.

Jason dropped the gym clothes and peered into the shadows. "It almost looks like..." He pulled on a corner, but the thing didn't budge.

Eric stepped forward and he and Jason gripped the edges of the heavy mass. They dug their heels into the floor and pulled backward, sliding it off the stack. It hit the floor with a heavy thud, billowing up dust and a handful of dead bugs. Coughing, they dragged it from the storage room and out into the gym.

It was huge and made of a thick material that had managed to escape the floodwaters from its vantage point on top of the boxes. Shawn and Eric grabbed one end, and Jason the other, and each started walking backward. The others quickly grabbed an edge and did the same. Soon they were all standing around an enormous circle. Once-bright colors had faded over the years into muddled whispers. Each colored cloth arced toward the middle, all meeting at a white circle in the center. It had the appearance of a very large umbrella, or circus tent, with alternating yellow, red, green, and blue sections.

Angela whispered, "It's a parachute."

"A what?" Eric asked.

"A parachute. We like literally *just* talked about this. You would all grab an edge and throw your arms up, and then run inside and hold it down behind you, so it would poof up and hold the air in, and then you were all inside this cool dome."

"I have never in my life seen one of these fuckers," Jason said.

"Well, you missed out, motherfucker. This shit was *golden*," Shawn said.

Angela smiled, fingering the rough edges of the parachute. "We would get so excited when we saw them pulling this out of storage. Almost as good as when you saw your teacher wheel the TV cart in."

For a moment they all stood there, holding the edges of the long-past-its-prime parachute, and remembered simpler days when they didn't need to know what they wanted to do for the rest of their lives.

Shawn looked at Eric and smiled. Eric grinned, then looked at Jason.

"You thinking what I'm thinking?"

"Fuck yeah, I am. I don't know what to do but I'm in," answered Jason, who then looked at Doug. "You?"

"Ditto," said Doug, "Ang?"

"Yep," Angela said.

"Well, no one asked me, but I'm in!" Val said.

They spread out evenly along the edge of the canvas circle. Due to some stroke of horrible luck, Angela ended up between Jason and Doug. At least she had a green section; it was her favorite color. Shawn stood directly across the circle from Angela, also in front of a green section, with Val on his left in front of yellow and Eric on his right in front of red.

"Hold tight," said Valerie, "one person lets go and it fucks it all up."

"We know," Angela answered.

"Well, Jason might not know."

"Ok, Jason," Angela said. "You throw your hands up in the air but don't let go, ok? Then you run forward and sort of hold it behind you, then you sit down on the edge of it inside the bubble, so it stays all puffed up."

"Sounds easy enough," said Jason, winking at her and grabbing the yellow cloth in front of him.

"You got this," Angela said.

"On the count of three," interrupted Doug, clutching his red cloth.

"Wait do we *go* on three or do we say 'one, two, three' *then* go?" Jason asked.

Doug sighed, "Oh my god. Go on three, like normal fucking people."

"Excuse the fuck out of me. Who pissed in your Cheerios?"

"Okay, okay. Let's just go," Angela said.

"One."

They all bent over and grabbed the edge of the parachute in front of them.

"Two."

They stood up, holding onto the fabric.

"Three."

Six pairs of arms flung into the air, and the parachute billowed upward as they ran forward. Val tripped but managed to hold onto the fabric. Laughing, she was the last to sit on her piece of the parachute, making her also the last to see what happened.

# 7

They each sat on their section of the fabric with the colored pieces stretching out behind them and arching toward the ceiling. Their eyes squinted to try to adjust to the underside of the parachute. It wasn't simply light coming through the yellow, red, blue, and green colors, though there was no way that light filtered from the dark gym on the other side. It was *bright*. So bright it appeared whiter than white, which Angela knew didn't make any sense, but that's where she was. She couldn't see a sun or any other source of light. At first, she thought someone had to be playing a joke on them, shining a flashlight in their eyes, but it soon became clear that it wasn't a joke at all. They stared at the light, then slowly around at each other. Angela could only see Doug on her right, and Jason on her left. Everyone else was too far away to make out. Which didn't make sense, as the parachute had to only be about twenty feet across. In the space where her other friends should have been, stretched an endless light and a strange clicking noise that seemed to have no pattern or steadiness. It rose and fell in volume with no rhyme or reason. Angela couldn't tell where it was coming from; it seemed to originate *inside* her head. The air around them was clear and fresh, in direct opposition to the musty heat of the abandoned gymnasium.

And they were no longer sitting on the cold, wooden floor of the school. Beneath them was a thick, plush layer of what looked like grass. Green, thin blades swayed to an unseen wind, tinkling as they hit each other like small bells on a Christmas wreath. The grass seemed to stretch for miles, with no end in sight.

Angela called out across the distance, "Val!"

A muffled cry returned as if Val were in a closet a mile away, but it was *her* voice. Which meant she *was* still there, even if Angela couldn't see her.

Before Angela could call out to anyone else, they were suddenly on the other side of the parachute, standing in the middle of the dark gymnasium, as if they had never lifted the thing at all.

# 8

"What the fuck was that?" cried Doug, looking around at his friends, then staring at the strange fabric still in his clutches. He dropped the parachute and stepped back as if it had burned his skin.

The others followed, staring down at the cloth from a safe distance.

"What the *fuck* was in that weed?" yelled Val, glaring at Eric on the other side of the flattened parachute. "I told you before, you can't cut it with that weird shit."

"I swear to God I didn't. This wasn't me. *Or* my weed. This is fucking *acid* man," stammered Eric, still staring at the parachute lying limp on the floor.

"He's right," Doug said, "I didn't even smoke earlier, and I saw it."

"Same, so what the fuck was it? That makes no sense, did you have a flashlight?" Angela asked Doug.

"No, God. *No*. I'm just as confused as you are," he answered.

"And what was that noise? I swear if you're fucking with us, Jason," Shawn said.

Valerie agreed, "Oh my god, yes. This is *exactly* the kind of shit you'd pull."

"It wasn't *me*," Jason argued.

"So, what happened, then, huh? How are we standing there one minute then back out the next?" Angela yelled.

"I don't know!" Jason yelled back.

They stared at each other in silence until Val cleared her throat before saying, "Maybe I lifted the edge back up? I just... I just wanted out of there, guys."

"Well, I don't know what y'all are waiting for, I say we go back in and see what the hell is going on. Not like it can hurt anything," Shawn shrugged as he stepped forward and reached down for the green fabric. He picked it up and grinned. "Let's do this, then. Let's see what other trip Eric's weed has us on."

"I told you—" Eric argued.

"Yes, we know, I'm just saying there's no other explanation," Shawn said.

"Then how do you explain Doug and I still seeing it? *We* didn't smoke," Angela said.

"Yeah, but you were up there, breathing it all in. You were sitting right next to us. Look, I'm not mad at you, Eric. I'm just saying, this is the strangest and most amazing trip I've ever been on, so let's not waste it. Let's go back in." Shawn rolled the edges of the fabric between his hands.

"He's got a point," said Jason, stepping toward the parachute.

"I'm down," said Eric, as he grabbed the red fabric between Jason and Shawn.

Angela and Doug looked at each other. She glanced at Jason before shrugging and returning to her spot at the edge of the circle. Doug followed.

"So, yeah?" asked Val, bending down to pick up the yellow edge of the parachute in front of her.

"Yeah," they all answered in unison before laughing at each other. Anything to break the tension.

They counted to three and lifted the parachute again.

# 9

It must have been a fluke— the strange experience they all had the first time they sat beneath the parachute, Angela thought. The light was now gone, replaced by a dim, dark interior one would expect from the inside of an abandoned elementary gym in the middle of the night. But, just as before, Angela could only see Doug far off to her right, and Jason to her left. The distance didn't make sense to her at all. Just a few seconds before, she could see Shawn across the parachute from her and now she couldn't even see the other side. The parachute's dingy fabric extended behind her and crept out of sight above her head.

Something rumbled in the darkness, and a deep, grinding sigh echoed around them. Another rumble answered it, then another.

"Angela?" Jason whispered.

"Yeah?"

She searched for the rest of the parachute. Something caught Angela's eye above her, a movement in the shadows.

"What's going on?"

Angela didn't answer, still squinting into the dark interior.

"Look up!" Val yelled across the expanse, her voice reaching them as a small echo.

Above them, where only a moment ago nothing but a seemingly endless parachute and darkness resided, was a large, flat surface. Grainy and dark brown like wood, it seemed to have some sort of polish on it. Bursts of brightness glinted off as it shifted, reflecting an unknown light source.

The groaning noise they heard before was getting louder, and the ceiling seemed closer. Angela reached up and touched the cool surface. It was cold, and her fingertips sunk into it like the soft bottom of the water behind her house. She jerked her hand away, her fingers now covered with the same dark brown material, shining in the darkness. She smelled her hand and flinched as her stomach rolled. It was *exactly* like the soft bottom of the slough. It smelled of water, algae, and things hidden in damp darkness for far too long.

When she glanced up again, the ceiling hung just six inches from her face.

A muffled scream came across the vast emptiness. It sounded like Shawn, but Angela couldn't make out what he was trying to say.

Another scream, this time much closer.

"Someone fucking lift it," Doug cried.

Angela jerked her head around to where Doug sat. Or, where he *had* been sitting just a few seconds before. He was now crouched, his feet still covering the edge of the parachute. His hands pushed against the ceiling, failing to make purchase. Like trying to find the bottom of a bayou, his arms disappeared past his elbows.

Angela clenched her fists around the edge of the fabric and jerked up.

## 10

Doug stared at his hands in awe. They were clean, with no trace of the strange mucky slime. He chuckled nervously.

Shawn turned his palms up, searching for any trace of the stuff.

"What the..." Shawn laughed as he looked at Doug. "This is fucking *awesome*, man."

"So, who lifted it this time?" Val asked. "I was about to, but—"

"I did," Angela said as she dropped the edge of the parachute with a thud onto the gym floor. "I lifted it."

"What the hell *is* this thing?" Val kicked at the colorful fabric with the tip of her shoe.

"Oh, snap."

Angela turned around to see Doug staring up at the windows along the top of the gym wall. "What?"

"Look." Doug pointed to the light streaming through the windows.

"What? I don't— " Angela froze. The *light*. There was daylight streaming through the windows. But that was impossible, as it was nighttime. There was no way it could be that bright outside.

"Far out," Shawn whispered.

"We should leave, let's head back to your house," Angela begged. "This doesn't feel right." She wasn't sure what was happening, but she knew it wasn't a *good* thing. There was some far-out shit going on beneath the parachute. Tripping or not, she just wanted to leave.

"I say we go back under, see what else it can do," Shawn piped up.

"I agree," Eric said.

"Excuse me, do none of you see a problem with all of this?" asked Angela, gesturing to the parachute on the floor, then the bright windows.

"Girl, *chill*," Shawn said as he rolled his eyes.

Val sighed. "Let's take a vote, then. All in favor of going back under that parachute, raise your hand."

Shawn and Eric's hands shot up, followed reluctantly by Doug. Angela glared at him, but he just shrugged.

"What? I think it would be fun to see what else is under there. Assuming anything *is*. Worth a look, anyway, right?"

Angela kept her hand down. "Nope. No," She shook her head. "I say we leave."

Val walked to stand beside her best friend. "I'm with Angela."

"Well, I'm with the dudes, let's go!" shouted Jason as he high fived the other guys.

"Val, I appreciate you, but I think we're outnumbered here," Angela said.

"Righteous. We're going back in," Shawn laughed.

Angela turned and watched the daylight glint off the edges of the broken glass on the other side of the gym.

"Y'all can always wait outside," said Shawn, as he bent down to pick up the parachute.

Val looked at Angela with one eyebrow raised. "It's up to you."

Angela sighed and walked back toward the edge of the parachute. Her footsteps echoed on the wooden floor. "No, it's fine. I'm in."

The group gathered back to their original spots along the edge of the parachute, acknowledging some unspoken rule that they had chosen their positions, whatever was in store for them.

"Ready?" Shawn looked around the circle at everyone.

"Not really," Val answered. "But let's do this."

They each knelt and grabbed their section of the parachute, then stood back up.

"One," announced Eric, before turning to Shawn.

"Two," said Shawn as he nodded his head at Doug.

"Three," said Doug, and they all threw their hands into the air and ran forward, still gripping the edges behind them.

## 11

---

It wasn't bright like their very first trip, but they could still see more around them than they did with the descending muck from the black lagoon.

Cold air shuddered past Angela, brushing her ponytail across her shoulders with a soft caress. Her skin erupted in goosebumps and her heart fluttered in her chest. She could tell this one was going to be different. Not that the others had been normal in any way, but this would a different thing entirely. She could *feel* it.

In the distance, something creaked like a rusty hinge on a door. Angela could hear her dad saying, "Just a little WD-40'll fix her right up." That was his answer to everything. That, or duct tape.

A soft light seeped into the circle as the sound of the rusty hinge faded into silence. Angela blinked fast, staring in front of her. She glanced to her right at Jason, but he only stared at the space above them. She slowly followed his gaze. Instead of open air like the first time, or a descending muck like the second, there appeared to be a normal ceiling, like what would be in a home. Maybe an older home, or a cabin in the woods that had planks as a ceiling. Swirls of wood grain stood out in dark colors against the lighter wood. It wasn't as high as the first one appeared to be, either. Nor was it lowering in a steady descent to squish them, so that seemed to already be an immediate improvement.

Angela sighed with relief. Nothing to crush them, no strange clicking noises in her head. In fact, she could hear birds softly crying out to each other, and a dog barking in the distance.

"What the fuck is this?" Doug finally broke the silence.

*What the fuck*, indeed. Angela wasn't sure what it was, but it all looked better than a bayou bottom. Smelled better, too. Not that it was all perfume and roses, rather a slight musty scent permeated the air around them. Like an old library, or her grandma's closet.

Directly in front of her, a tattered rug lay splayed out over a wooden floor. The wood seemed to be an exact replica of the ceiling above them. A wooden bed sat half on the rug and half off, with bright white sheets tucked in tightly. A single, small, white pillow clung to the top of the sheets. Next to the bed was a wooden nightstand, an old one that looked like it belonged in a museum instead of someone's bedroom. A golden clock sat on top of the nightstand beneath a glass case, the bottom spinning as the second hand ticked. The wall behind the bed and nightstand was covered in wallpaper, white and pink flowers on a brown background. Very 1970's, in Angela's opinion.

The same pattern covered another wall directly across from them, and a single wooden door occupied the middle. The wall stretched out to meet another wall with a nightstand and bed sitting against it on the right, and another wall with a dresser on the left. But there wasn't a fourth wall one would expect in a bedroom. Instead, the two sides curved around Jason, Angela, and Doug, meeting in the middle and blending somehow. It was strange, and not like any room Angela could ever remember seeing. The soft fabric of the parachute remained beneath them, but only the edges appeared beneath the wall.

Shawn, Val, and Eric weren't there.

Angela called out, hoping they were just out of sight like the previous times, "Val!"

A return cry answered from beyond the door on the opposite wall. Angela stood up and took a step away from the fabric.

"Don't!" Doug cried out, afraid of what might happen if they stopped touching the parachute.

Angela froze. After nothing happened, she continued walking forward. Doug and Jason slowly rose to their feet without taking their eyes off the small yellow and red fabric, as if it would slip away forever.

The floor beneath Angela gave slightly as she walked like it wasn't fully supported from below. She turned the doorknob and pulled. Val stood on the other side, with her hand also on the knob. She had had the same idea. The girls smiled at each other.

"This is so cool," Val said.

"I don't know about 'cool.' What's on your side?" Angela said.

"Looks like a bedroom." Val poked her head further into Angela's room, peering around Doug and Jason. "Exactly like this one. Weird."

"We left weird behind a long time ago. This is... *insane*," said Angela, laughing.

Val stepped back to let Angela walk into the other room, followed by the guys. It was identical to the first room, complete with a short fringe of parachute sticking out where the wallpaper met the floor.

"Yo, this is some sick shit, right?" Eric asked.

Jason and Doug nodded in agreement.

"Yours has a hole in the floor," Jason said.

"Yeah, looks like stairs," Eric said.

"Well, what are we standing *here* for? Let's go!" Before anyone could reply, Doug climbed down into the hole. As his head bounced lower with each step, Val leaned down into the darkness and cupped her hands around her mouth.

"What is it? Is it safe?"

"Totally!" said Doug, his voice seeping upward and echoing off the wood around them.

One by one, the rest of the group stepped down into the lower level, following Doug's lead. There was a small landing after a few steps, then the staircase twisted at a hard right angle, leading further down. Angela made it to the bottom, then stepped out onto a thin, carpet-covered floor. Shawn and Eric poked their heads through a door on the right, and Doug opened a door on their left. Unlike the upper rooms, the small space in front of the stairs had four complete walls without any parachute fabric showing through.

"Should we maybe stay together?" Angela hesitated.

"It's fine, quit worrying," Jason said.

Shawn and Eric disappeared into another room, and Angela stepped aside to allow Val and Jason space to leave the stairway.

Doug gestured toward Angela. "Let's check this one out."

She glanced at Jason before following Doug through the open doorway on the left. Val and Jason joined them. It looked like a kitchen; a musty, unused, and very old kitchen, but a standard kitchen. A wooden dining table with four matching chairs occupied a rug in the middle of the room. Against a wall on her left sat a metal stove. Doug was trying to open the oven door, but it didn't budge.

"It won't open."

"Let me try," Jason said.

"What, like you're stronger? I'm telling you, it won't open," Doug said.

Jason pulled on the door, but it didn't move. He yanked harder.

"What the—" Jason jumped back, confused, as the entire stove tipped over onto the floor.

"It's hollow," said Val, as she examined the oven. "Completely hollow. The door is *painted* on."

"This is wild, man," Jason said.

They looked around at the rest of the items in the room. Angela ran her hand along a white refrigerator door.

"It's wood. Painted wood."

"Who makes a refrigerator out of *wood*?" Doug asked.

"The same person who glues plates to a table?" asked Val, as she tugged on a red plate sitting on the dining table.

A countertop edged up to the far wall, and a window had been cut into the wallpapered space above a sink. Beneath the counter were closed cabinets and, peeking out below those, was their parachute. It lay as it had in the rooms upstairs, cut off by the wall, but the colorful folds were still visible, enough to get her fingers around, anyway.

Angela stepped forward and peered through the window. "Y'all..." she whispered.

Looking out from the kitchen window was another, much larger room. A child's room, judging from the Care Bear bedding and toys piled on the floor. Past the bed was a large open door, but she couldn't see anything on the other side.

Val gasped behind Angela. "Is that..."

"A kid's bedroom," Angela answered. She stepped aside so Doug and Jason could see for themselves.

Val and Angela looked at each other, then glanced at the door they had just stepped through. As if they had the idea at the same time, they moved quickly to the door, through the small opening in front of the stairs, and into the room where Shawn and Eric had disappeared. It was set up like a living room. The wallpaper was different but looked equally as old. Green squares intersected with maroon and yellow lines in the ugliest plaid pattern Angela had ever seen. A plush, red velvet couch sat flush with one wall, and two matching chairs had been placed on the opposite side, facing it. On the wall directly in front of the girls was another window. Bright parachute fabric filled the space where the wall met the wooden planks on the floor. Shawn and Eric were blocking the view, preventing her from seeing if there was another child's room on the other side or something completely different. At that point, anything seemed possible.

"Yo Eric, you gotta come see this," said Doug, as he and Jason entered the room behind them.

Eric and Shawn turned around, surprised to see everyone standing there.

Angela stepped up to the window. A wall in the distance matched the bright blue wall on the other side by the bed. Big, white letters hung from yellow ribbons against the wall, spelling out the name "KELLY." Flower stickers adorned every other letter.

"It's a kid's room," Angela whispered.

"How do you figure that?" Eric asked.

"The other side. There's a bed and toys and everything."

"We're in a giant kid's room," Val agreed.

"No fucking way," Shawn said.

"Go see."

Shawn and Eric disappeared through the doorway. Their footsteps rumbled along the wooden floor, briefly stopped, then came back toward the rest of the group. They stopped to catch their breath, their eyes wide with wonder.

"How?" Shawn asked.

Val touched the red velvet fabric on the couch before sitting down. She jiggled, then settled into the seat. It seemed like it was strong enough to hold her weight.

"Holy shit," Val said.

"What?" Angela turned from the window. Val stared at a space in the shadow behind the open door.

"Ok, don't freak out," she whispered, "but someone is sitting behind the door."

Everyone in the room froze and slowly turned their heads. A figure faced the wall, half-hidden by the open door. Perfect ringlets of black hair cascaded down its back. A white dress, tied at the waist with a large white bow, covered the girl from her neck to her ankles. She sat on a glossy black bench facing a black piano. Val stepped closer as Angela held her breath.

She touched the white fabric dress, then pushed. The figure fell over onto the floor, black button eyes staring up at the ceiling from a dark brown cotton face. A black marker-dotted nose, and a thin line of red string bowed into a smile, made up the rest of the face. It was a doll, as tall as any of them, though thinner.

Angela reached over the bench and touched a white key on the piano, expecting a characteristic "plink," but nothing sounded from the wooden keys as she tried to press them. More fake props.

Val looked at the doll on the floor in front of them, then

over at the window and through the door into the other room. "It's a *dollhouse*."

"I think you're right," said Angela, as she ran her hand along the edge of the piano.

"We're in a *doll*house?" Jason asked.

Doug sat down on one of the red chairs and stared at the doll on the floor.

"This is fucking gnarly, man," Shawn said.

Val returned to her seat on the couch, shaking her head. "How is this possible?"

Angela eased down next to her, and the couch creaked beneath the added weight. "No idea," she said.

"We should go back," said Jason, as he walked toward the open door.

"Not yet," Doug said. "Let's hang out here for a minute. How many people can say they've been inside a dollhouse? *No one* is going to believe us."

"I guess, what's a few more minutes going to hurt?" Jason turned back to the room.

Heavy thudding interrupted them, and the house shook slightly in rhythm. A shadow filled the window and then disappeared. The same creaking noise from earlier returned, like rusty hinges in need of WD-40. An entire wall pulled away as harsh light replaced the soft glow from before, filling the small space and leaving nothing in shadow.

Val screamed as a giant white hand reached through the space where a wall had been just seconds before. Angela flew off the couch and ran toward the door while Eric and Shawn came running from the other side. They collided with her and Jason, and everyone fell in a tangle of legs and arms. As they were climbing back to their feet, Shawn screamed.

"Val!"

Angela turned around in time to see the hand pluck Val from the couch as if she were a doll and carry her back through the bright space. The wall returned with a creak and the light faded once again to a soft glow. On the other side of the wall, Val screamed, followed by a thumping noise. Small footsteps hurried around the side of the dollhouse to the window facing them. It was Val, cradling her left arm against her chest and crying. Angela ran forward and jerked on the windowsill, but it wouldn't open. The others joined her, and Shawn took off one of his shoes and tried to break the window, crying, "Val, stand back!"

On the third blow, the hard plastic window popped out in one piece and clattered to the wooden floor of the wrap-around porch. Shawn and Angela reached toward Val to pull her through.

## 12

The gym was dark once again, with only the faint glow of moonlight whispering through the broken window. For a moment it all seemed so... *normal*. It was just Polk Elementary. They were just hanging out like they always did, though inside the gym instead of on top of the roof.

But Val was no longer with them.

Shawn shattered the silence, screaming as he looked around at the others, his eyes wild, "Who lifted it? Who?? Why?!"

The parachute lay at their feet, deflated and lifeless.

Jason took a deep breath, "I think it was me."

"Why would you do that? We almost had her!" Shawn cried.

"I don't know. One minute I was standing by the wall and my foot got caught under the edge of the parachute, so I moved it, and..."

"We have to go back," screamed Shawn, dropping to the floor, and grabbing the green canvas.

Doug ran across the parachute and leaned down, jerking

the fabric out of Shawn's hands. He dropped it on the floor and looked down at Shawn, still crouching.

"Just hold on. We go to a different place every time. How do we even find her?"

Shawn jumped to his feet and balled his fists. He took a step toward Doug, his eyes wide and bloodshot. "It's your fucking fault! You're the one that wanted to stay longer!"

Shawn swung his right fist, hitting Doug on the side of his jaw. Doug dropped to his knees with a hard thud on the wooden floor. His hand flew to his face, and he looked up at Shawn incredulously.

"What the fuck, man?"

Shawn shook his hand then clenched it again as he took another step toward Doug.

Doug held his arms up. "I'm sorry, but how was I supposed to know a giant hand was gonna grab her? Dude! Seriously, stop!"

"Stop!" Eric jumped between them, facing Shawn. "We'll go back in. She'll be there, she *has* to be." Shawn stared at him until the rage drained from his face, then he sighed and looked at Doug.

"Sorry, man."

Doug nodded and climbed to his feet, still rubbing his jaw. "It's cool."

Angela and Jason watched in silence. She was also mad at Doug for wanting to stay, not that she would start a fist-fight with him over it, but he *was* the one who wanted to stay longer.

"Okay, hold on let's think..." Eric said. "Jason, you said your foot was under the parachute. So... it was along that one wall. Our feet must have all been touching it when we were trying to get Val through the window."

"What does that matter?" said Shawn, pacing the gym floor and stopping every few feet to glare at Doug.

"Well, it matters if we want to all come back next time. Let's figure this thing out. There has to be some kinda rules, right?" Eric said.

"He's right," said Angela, as she walked across the canvas toward them. "We were all touching the parachute edge except for Val when Jason lifted it."

Jason, still standing on the other side of the parachute, lowered his head.

"I know you didn't *mean* to, but that's what fucking happened, okay? That must mean—"

"It means you left my sister!" Shawn yelled at Jason.

"Dude, I'm *sorry*."

"This isn't going to bring her back," Angela said. "Let's keep a straight head here so we can figure out *how* to get her back. We all had our feet touching the parachute when Jason lifted it."

Shawn stopped pacing and sighed. "Yes."

"But *I* wasn't," Eric said. "I wasn't as close to the wall as y'all were."

"But you were touching *me*," Shawn said. "I felt you behind me, your hand was on my back."

"Okay so..."

"We have to be touching the parachute, or *each other,* to come back?" Angela asked.

"Well, Val wasn't touching it," Shawn said. "And *she's not here* so..."

"Ok, so this is all we know. We have to go with it," Angela said. "Shawn, we're not leaving her, I promise. We're going to find her."

Shawn nodded. "How?"

"We go back," Angela said.

They gathered around the limp parachute once again, each person seeming to automatically go to the same color section as they had before. Angela stood in front of green, Doug on her right in front of red, Jason on her left in front of yellow. Across from her, she could easily see Shawn standing in front of another green section. She knew, once they were beneath the parachute, she wouldn't be able to see him or Eric. Something *happened* to the space in between, and it terrified her. She didn't understand how everything expanded so much once they were inside that she couldn't see across the parachute. Or once they were *under*? Within? Fuck if she knew what to call whatever it was they were experiencing. It was fucking *weird*.

Maybe it was all a dream. Either that, or the strangest trip any of them had ever been on, but Angela leaned toward it being a dream. That was the only logical explanation.

Her eyes fluttered to the empty, yellow cloth next to Shawn and she quickly looked away. They would get Val back. They *had* to. Or, she would wake up in her own bed at her own house and this would all go away.

Angela took a deep breath and lifted the parachute without counting down, closely followed by the others in a soft, undulating wave.

## 13

No longer expecting any sort of normalcy, Angela was still shocked to find herself underwater. She held onto the parachute as they sank into the murky darkness, drifting feet-first down through the water. Angela wasn't sure what weighed them down, she was typically what her mom liked to call a floater. She always had to kick like crazy to stay beneath the surface, yet there she was, stiff as a board, and steadily sinking.

Above her, the water stretched for what seemed like miles. Angela watched her bubbles rise and caught sight of a flutter of fabric high above them. She glanced first at Doug, then at Jason, both looking around their own sections trying to figure out what was going on. As before, Angela could no longer see Eric or Shawn, but she figured they had to be close by.

A light appeared far below them, darting back and forth like a firefly in the woods. Soon it was joined by another, and then another until a symphony of lights danced below their feet. Angela still couldn't figure out what produced the glow, since nothing could be seen but miles of dark water above them, below them, and on either side. Behind them, the parachute rippled in the water as it rose and disappeared into the darkness above. Her lungs burned in her chest, aching for oxygen. She was about to lift the edge of the parachute when a blur of movement caught her eye. Angela's heart fluttered.

*Val.*

Maybe she found her way back to the group.

But as the shape grew closer, she realized it was Shawn. What was he doing away from the edge of the parachute? He knew the dangers, or as much as any of them knew at that point, anyway. Either way, it couldn't be good. Angela held onto the fabric with one hand and gestured toward Shawn to come closer with the other. Doug and Jason both held onto their pieces, straining to hold their breath as they all continued sinking. No one dared to lift the parachute. Jason, especially, wouldn't make that mistake again.

Shawn reached Doug first, grabbing the edge of the parachute next to him like a lifeline. That meant Eric was still on the other side, now alone. Angela pointed across the emptiness and looked at Shawn, her eyebrows raised. He gave her a thumbs-up, whatever that fucking meant.

The seconds stretched behind Angela like hours, and her lungs felt every bit of it. As they sank closer to the lights below, shapes appeared around each bright spot. Angela rubbed her eyes and looked again. She didn't know if it was the water blurring her vision, but she thought she could see... it couldn't be...

Blurred objects morphed into solid, enormous creatures. A tangle of tentacles stretched out from their bulbous bodies. They were clear, with skin like a used condom stretched across a jumble of pulsating organs and what looked like blue blood vessels. She didn't know where their eyes were, or what any other part of their body was. Each tentacle stretched about ten feet from the body, covered in the same clear skin. There were no organs in the tentacles, only blue and white lines throughout, leading to a bright tip, the source of each light they had seen from above. Angela didn't stop to count, but it looked like more tentacles than any octopus she knew. Not that she knew a lot of octopi, but she had seen her fair share of National Geographic episodes. Then there was that time her seventh grade class went to see "Oceans: The Source of Life" at the Imax Theatre in Galveston. Mr. Hinkles would shit his pants if he saw what was in front of them now.

Beneath the creatures were more blurred shapes, shifting between even more spots of light. And, below those, more muted, fuzzy circles of light darted back and forth in the depths. Angela glanced at the others. They appeared mesmerized by the lights and strange creatures. She returned her gaze to a tentacle almost within her reach. As she drifted further down, she could see it wasn't just a glowing ball at the end of the creature's appendages. It was an open mouth. The glow came from within the throat of each tentacle, and the wide mouth projected that light around three rows of razor-sharp teeth—

## 14

"What the *hell* was that?" screamed Eric, inches from Shawn's face. "You just swim off into whatever that shit was? We could have lost *you*, too!" He pushed Shawn away from him.

"I thought," Shawn stammered. "I thought I saw her." His shoulders slumped forward, and he sighed.

"Look man, you could have killed yourself," Eric put both hands on Shawn's shoulders and looked him in the eyes. "You've got to get it together, okay?" His hands met behind Shawn's neck, and he pulled him closer. The two hugged while Eric whispered, "We'll find her. We'll find her."

The others stared at them. Angela knew there was zero chance Val could be in that water. No one could possibly believe she would be there, fighting for air or surviving those... whatever the hell those things were.

"You saw her?" Angela asked.

Shawn wiped his face and cleared his throat, "I don't know, man. I saw *something*. Or a shadow, maybe, of something."

Angela dropped down to the cold gym floor and pulled her knees to her chest. She wrapped her arms around her legs and rested her forehead on them. It was impossible. The entire thing was impossible, and their chances of finding Val...

"It's gonna be okay Ang," Jason whispered as he crouched down next to her and put a warm hand on her back.

Angela lifted her chin and faced him. She brushed the back of her hand across her cheeks, wiping the tears away, but more had already taken their place before she was done.

"You don't know that."

"You're right, I don't," replied Jason, still resting his hand on her lower back, "but I have to believe we'll find her. Otherwise..."

Doug sat down on the other side of Angela, glaring at Jason before leaning in and wiping away her tears. "We'll find her. I promise you."

Jason stood up and brushed himself off.

Shawn pulled away from Eric and cleared his throat, "Okay, so let's go back in. We're getting her back." A new resolve showed on his face, and his eyes narrowed. He had changed. It wasn't a version of Shawn that Angela had ever seen before. He was laid back, usually high. Not angry, and definitely not the type to go around punching people or screaming.

Doug stood and held out his hand to Angela. She grabbed it to pull herself up from the floor, and they walked back to the edge of the god-forsaken bit of cloth on the gym floor.

Shawn pulled up the edge with both hands and looked around at the others. Reluctantly, they picked up the edge of the cloth in front of them. Shawn counted to three, and they lifted the parachute again.

## 15

The second the fabric cleared their heads, they were falling.

Angela scrambled to hold onto the thin cloth as her legs dangled above a pit, the bottom of which she couldn't see, only more darkness below her. The air was foggy and freezing, a cold unlike anything Angela had ever experienced. It stung her skin as if someone had slapped her. Her fingers burned as they clutched the fabric, and a crackling came from her right. Doug clung to the parachute, staring down at his legs in horror.

She didn't have long to figure out why he was terrified, as a white-hot pain inched up Angela's own feet, encircling her ankles and reaching up to her calves. She could no longer move her feet. When the ice climbed above her knees and kissed the bottom of her green shorts, she tried to scream but inhaled air so cold, it burned her throat and lungs. Panicked, she looked to her left at Jason. As if in a silent film, he gestured and tried to speak but the only sound was the snapping of ice around them.

As she watched, Jason's legs snapped off with a ferocious

crack, flinging frozen chunks of jeans and flesh into the air as they plummeted into the depths below. Tears had solidified on the edges of his wide eyes, and his mouth lay open in shock. Angela glanced down again at her legs and the pain emanating from them. The fabric still swayed above them, and Angela's cold fingers ached as she struggled to hold on. She kicked her legs to try to get a better grip; she needed to lift the edge of the parachute. As she kicked again, a searing pain consumed her knees and bile rose in the back of her throat. Her legs, as with Jason's, had also broken off with a snap and fallen into the pit below them.

If *her* legs had frozen... a quick glance at Doug told her all she needed to know. The ice climbed up his torso and passed his waist. Everything below that was gone, leaving only jagged ripped flesh as if a child had tried to tear apart a loaf of bread with his hands.

They were dying. Literally freezing to death.

The cold inched toward Angela's waist and the air around her flickered and pulsated as if she were being shaken. The room went dark, and the parachute slipped to the edge of her fingertips...

## 16

Angela sat on the gym floor, gasping for breath, and touching her arms, her waist, and her legs. Everything was there again, all limbs accounted for, all with warm blood coursing through them. She no longer shivered from the cold, no longer felt the pain of her limbs freezing and falling into the nothingness below as they detached from her body. She glanced around the edges of the parachute. Eric and Shawn huddled together, eyes wide and silent. Jason stood at the edge of the fabric, staring at her, eyebrows raised. She nodded; she was okay. Doug ran to her and leaned down, pulling her into an embrace.

"Are you ok?" he asked, when he finally stepped back.

"I am. I think," Angela answered, shaking from the memory of the cold though the gym was balmy and warm. "You?"

"Yeah."

Angela laid on her back on the hard floor, staring at the ceiling. The perfectly normal, gray gym ceiling. She focused on breathing in, then out. She wiggled her toes and fingers, still not believing they were all there, and at their normal temperature. They weren't even tingling, like what happened when her foot would fall asleep in Chemistry class and the blood would all rush back through her veins as she stood up.

It was as if nothing had happened at all. Like the frozen cavern didn't exist and her body had never known the horrors within.

"So," Shawn said. "What happens in there isn't *real*?"

"I think so," said Jason, shaking his head in disbelief.

"Val might be okay, then, once we get her back out here. Right?"

"I don't know man, but sure. I mean, look what happened to us just now," Jason said.

Angela didn't need to ask what had happened to Shawn and Eric, who were on the other side of the parachute and out of sight once inside. She could see the shock on their faces and knew they had gone through the same thing.

"Ok, let's go back," said Shawn, as he returned to his strip of green fabric.

"Wait a second," Doug argued. "Are you fucking with me? I'm not going back in there!"

"We have to! Val's there! *My sister* is in there!" Shawn yelled back.

"It's too dangerous, can't you see that? Do you wanna get us *all killed*?" Doug asked.

Eric glared at Doug as he walked to his strip of red parachute. "I'm not giving up. I'm with you, Shawn."

Doug threw his hands in the air, "We could have all *died*!"

"But we didn't. We're fine. Nothing is real in there, right?" Shawn's jaw was firm, and his hands held tightly to the fabric. He frowned at Doug. "So stay, then. No one is making you go back. But I'm going."

Angela didn't hesitate. "Me, too."

Val was her best friend. She couldn't just leave her in there. She turned to stare at Jason.

"Me, too," said Jason, as he leaned down to pick up his section of yellow cloth.

"Angela, think about this! You could *die*! We don't know what else is under there!" Doug gestured to the parachute laying on the floor.

She moved away, eyes fixating on the parachute in front of her. "I'm going."

Doug stared at her in silence. No one spoke as he sighed, then walked to his red section of fabric.

"Fine, let's just get in, get Val, and get out before we all get killed."

"Eric, whatever happens, you stay with the parachute, okay?" Shawn said.

"What? Why?" Eric asked.

"Just in case we have to leave in a hurry. We can all hold hands but, that way, only the first person has to get to you. Like a safety chain."

"Okay but I don't like it. I'd rather be out there with you." Eric frowned, then continued, "but if you think it'll help..."

"It will. I think," Shawn sighed. "I don't really know, but maybe."

Without counting, they all lifted the parachute above their heads.

## 17

The parachute cleared the top of Angela's head with a gust of air and the end of her ponytail whipped around her face. As she pulled the fabric back down behind her and sat on the edge, she looked around. There was a floor. That much was a plus, especially given the endless pit of climbing ice they had experienced before, but it wasn't the gym floor. Instead, a soft, gray and green moss-like substance covered everything. It was spongy and gave slightly when Angela sat down. At least it was comfortable, if not slightly cool to the touch.

The floor stretched out as far as she could see, interspersed every few feet with a puddle of stagnant water. It smelled like an aquarium that hadn't been cleaned in two years. Old, musty water and dead fish. Like the descending, mushy ceiling from before.

Nothing clicked or creaked in the space, only silence. A low haze hung over them and the air was thick and heavy. Angela stood up, exerting too much effort for such a simple task. It was almost as if something pushed *down* on her, preventing her from standing too quickly. Like the gravity was off. On either side of her, Doug and Jason also struggled to stand up.

She ignored it. Nothing surprised her inside the parachute anymore.

As Angela brushed green moss from her legs, she saw a figure in the distance. She squinted as it came closer. Her heart dropped as she realized it couldn't be Val, the person (or thing?) was much too tall to be her best friend.

Shawn.

He walked slower than usual as if he were carrying a heavy load. By the time he reached the three of them, he was bent over and gasping for breath.

"Okay," He gasped as he pointed behind him. "Eric stayed." He took another shaky breath before saying, "Let's go find Val."

"What's wrong? Are you okay?" Doug asked.

"Yeah, just... heavy, man. Heavy," Shawn answered.

"I think the gravity is different here," said Angela, having no real knowledge of physics, but she watched enough movies to get an idea of what might be happening to them. If that place even had similar physics or gravity. Hell, for all she knew, they'd all get flung off into space any minute. Anything seemed possible.

The others nodded and joined hands. Whatever happened, they would stay together. The group walked away from the edge of the parachute with Shawn in the lead, then Doug and Angela, and Jason bringing up the rear. As they pushed forward, every movement became a chore. Her entire body felt heavier like she was wearing the ankle weights her mom used to wear around the house.

A sadness fell over Angela, and helplessness filled her thoughts, slowing her even further. She stopped, her hand jerking out of Doug's as he moved forward without her. Jason bumped into her back.

"What is it?" Doug asked as he looked back, reaching for her hand.

"I don't know. What's the point? We aren't going to find her," Angela cried, letting the tears cut paths through the dust and dirt on her face. She eased herself down onto the mossy ground.

"What's the *point*?" Shawn stopped and turned back to the group. "Are you fucking kidding me?"

"I don't know man, I'm with her," whispered Jason as he sat down next to her. "Nothing matters." He looked down at his hands as if they belonged to someone else.

"I don't know what's going on with you guys, but we aren't giving up," said Shawn, his voice catching on the last word.

Doug joined Angela on the ground, sitting close but not touching her. He glanced out into the nothingness that stretched before them. Just a gray and green world full of spongy moss, stagnant water, and a boggy stench that permeated everything.

Angela could feel it on her skin, a prickly numbness crawling up her neck. A sadness unlike anything she had ever experienced. She just wanted to be alone. To be sitting there, by herself, so she could go to sleep and never wake up again. Never have to deal with it all. She wanted to be *done*. Angela glanced down at her wrist; at the braided metal bracelet her dad had made for her years before. She removed it and flipped it over, found the rough edge, and started sawing at the delicate skin on the inside of her left wrist.

"What the fuck?" Doug asked, slightly louder than a whisper. He moved in slow motion, grabbing her hand as she pulled away from the trickling blood and tried to move the bracelet to her other wrist.

Angela looked up at Doug, tears still streaming down her face. He kept a tight grip on her bloody wrist and cried, "No."

Jason slowly climbed to his feet and said, "We have to go back."

He grabbed Doug's hand and pulled him to a standing position. Shawn turned to look in the direction they had been walking, then slowly nodded in agreement. Jason took off his shirt and knelt to wrap it around the cut on Angela's wrist, then helped her stand. Everyone joined hands again as they turned around to head back to the parachute.

The walk felt like forever, but probably only took a few minutes. Every step was harder than the previous one. Every step made Angela alternate between going out of her mind and wanting to lie back down on the soft ground and never get up. She was so *tired*. It took all her energy to put one foot in front of the other and allow herself to be pulled forward by Doug. Jason kept his hand on her back, pushing with each half-step she took. Everyone kept their heads down, occasionally turning their face to the inside of their arm and trying to wipe away tears without letting go of each other.

Shawn broke the silence, crying out as he dropped Doug's hand and surged forward with every ounce of energy he could muster. Angela couldn't see what he had reacted to, the dense fog only allowed for a few feet of visibility. By the time they caught up to him, she couldn't believe what lay in front of her.

Eric.

Sweet, intelligent, and perpetually high Eric, lying motionless on his side. A dark red slit in his throat had already crusted over. Dried blood covered his neck and the top of his shirt. Lying a few inches away from his hand was his belt, the buckle covered with his blood. There's no way he could have done what he did and had the blood dry as completely as it had in the time they were gone. In normal circumstances, anyway. But who knew what the hell happened in that place?

"Oh my god," Angela whispered. "What..."

"Grab onto each other," Shawn tried to yell but his voice came out hoarse and pale. "Now!"

Jason grabbed Angela's hand. She held onto Doug with her other hand, and he squeezed Shawn's arm. Shawn had one hand on Eric and, with the other, lifted the edge of the blood-stained parachute next to Eric's body.

# 18

Shawn screamed as he shook Eric's limp body.

The cut on Eric's neck was gone, replaced by smooth brown skin. His shirt had also been renewed, lacking any bloody evidence of what had happened beneath the parachute. He looked like he could be taking a nap or had simply passed out from drinking too much Everclear.

Jason pulled Shawn away, keeping his arm around Shawn's chest and holding him tightly.

"He's gone," Jason whispered. "He's gone."

Shawn finally stopped fighting and fell limp in Jason's arms. He slumped to the floor, pulling Jason down with him. Shawn clung to his friend as if he were a buoy in the middle of the Gulf of Mexico. He leaned his head on Jason and wept silently.

Doug put his arm around Angela. She jumped, unaware he had been standing so close to her. She moved closer and they both stared at Eric. His arms were splayed out unnaturally, and one lay half on top of the faded red fabric of the parachute.

"Why didn't he..." Angela said.

"Get fixed?" Doug asked.

"Yeah. Like before, with the ice." She looked down at her wrist, free from blood or cuts. Her smooth olive skin looked the exact way it had that morning when she woke up. Jason's shirt was back on his body, free of her blood like it had never been wrapped around her wrist.

"I don't know," Doug said. "Maybe because he was dead when we lifted the edge?" Doug kicked the parachute in disgust. "I don't know, I don't know what the fucking rules are to this shit."

"With the ice..." Shawn cleared his throat as he lifted his head from Jason's embrace. "Do y'all remember coming back? Like, you were alive when you came back?"

"Yeah," Doug said, "barely. Like a chicken that runs around even after his head is chopped off."

"Same here," Jason said.

"Same," Angela agreed.

"So," Shawn said as he pulled away from Jason and stood up, staring at Eric again. His voice caught in his throat. He took a deep breath and pulled his gaze away from his dead friend, "so maybe that's why. If you're alive at all when you come back, you're... healed? But if you die in there..."

"What is this, fucking *Nightmare on Elm St.*?" asked Doug, getting more pissed off by the minute.

No one answered him. They didn't know anything about the parachute or what the hell happened beneath it.

"We need help. Like, real help," Doug said.

"Who's going to believe this?" said Angela, as she threw her hand toward the parachute, then Eric's body.

"I don't know but we're clearly in over our heads," Doug said. "I'll go, you guys stay with Eric."

"And Val," Shawn said.

"What?"

"And Val. Eric and *Val*. She's still out there, or did you already forget?" Shawn seethed.

Doug stared at him. "Of course, I didn't forget."

He broke eye contact with Shawn and reached a hand out to Angela, asking, "Want to come with me?"

"No, I'll stay here."

"Okay. Shawn, do you have the keys to Val's van?"

"No. They're in her pocket, I guess." He turned to look down at the parachute. "Wherever that is."

"Well fuck," Doug sighed. "Does anyone know how to hot wire a car?"

"What kind of skills do you think I've been hiding from you all these years?" Angela asked.

"Nothing, never mind. Okay, I'm going to get help even if I have to walk. Surely one of these houses down the street will let me use their phone." Doug waved to the group and started walking across the empty gymnasium to the window they had climbed through. He stopped after a few steps and turned around, staring specifically at Angela. "Do *not* go back in there."

She nodded her head and watched him turn back and start walking.

Once Doug was out of earshot, Shawn whispered, "I'm going back. I'm not leaving Val in there to die. Come with me or not, I don't care."

"I'm coming," Angela said. She couldn't leave her friend in that place.

Jason studied Angela for a second before agreeing.

They shuffled to their sections and quietly lifted the edge of the parachute. Doug never turned around.

# 19

The air steamed and split around them, crackling like a TV with bad reception. Angela gasped as a loud, piercing noise consumed her, tumbling into her brain like an avalanche. An intense pain hit her like lightning, and it seemed every cell in her body was on fire. Next to her, Jason had doubled over with one hand over his ears, screaming. The other clutched the edge of the parachute with white knuckles. He shimmered like a heatwave over an asphalt road in August.

Angela lifted the edge—

## 20

Angela moaned and held her head in her hands, trying to squeeze out the memory of the noise.

"What the hell—," Shawn asked, shaking his head back and forth.

"—was that?" Jason finished.

"Yeah," said Shawn, taking a deep breath.

"Val wasn't there," Angela said.

"What?" Jason said

"Val wasn't in there."

"How could you even tell? We were there for like, half a second," Jason said.

"Guys," Shawn interrupted.

"I just know," Angela answered.

"Fine."

"*Guys!*"

Jason and Angela finally turned to Shawn. He stared at Doug's back. Doug, who was still only a third of the way to the broken window they had first climbed through.

"What the..." Angela tilted her head.

As they watched, Doug slowly lifted his foot and his body shifted forward.

Angela ran up to him, but he acted like he couldn't see her.

"Doug," cried Angela, reaching out to touch his shoulder, but her hand kept going when it should have come into contact with his shirt. She flayed her hand in the air through his back, as if Doug were a projection instead of a living, breathing person. Confused, Angela moved around in front of him. He stared straight ahead as if she weren't there at all. His back foot lifted off the wooden floor agonizingly slowly, and his knee bent. His eyes remained forward, focused on the broken window. His face, smooth as a baby's ass just a few minutes before they went beneath the parachute, now had a beard poking through. Angela hated his stubble, it always chafed her when they were kissing. He kept it short and shaved it every single day to prevent it from getting prickly, just for her.

Doug's back leg inched forward. Shawn reached out to lay a hand on Doug's shoulder, but his hand went through Doug like a fog, and he fell forward into and straight through his friend. Shawn tumbled to the ground, then jumped to his feet and skittered backward away from Doug, who was still standing and looking forward, as if nothing had happened at all. As if they had just gone to the edge of the parachute a few seconds before.

Angela reached out to Doug again, but her hands went through him like a dream, a hazy mist. But there wasn't anything hazy about him. He was just Doug. If Doug were moving at the speed of snail and somehow had a five-o-clock shadow.

"How long were we gone?" Jason asked

"Not *this* long," Angela peered into Doug's eyes, staring

straight through her. "No way it was this long. Look at his face. It's like we were in there for days, not seconds."

Shawn leaned closer to Doug's chest and cocked his head to the side. "I think he's still breathing." He managed a half-smile toward Angela. "At least there's that."

Jason shook his head in confusion. "Maybe we fucked something up in that last place? Maybe we should go back in."

"No," Angela cried. "We need help. Like, adult help. We're in over our heads, here."

"What are you suggesting, then?" Jason asked *"Going for help*? That didn't exactly work out for Doug."

"Yes, that's exactly what I'm saying. We *all* go, so this," Angela gestured at Doug's body stuck in time, "doesn't happen."

"No, the fuck we aren't," Shawn snapped. "You want to just leave Val trapped in there? Leave Eric dead on the floor?" Shawn glanced back at Eric's body lying next to the parachute. His voice cracked as he continued, "No." He shook his head and repeated, "NO."

"He's right," Jason said.

Angela turned to Jason, surprised. He held her gaze without blinking.

She sighed. "Okay, let's get Val. It's not like Doug's going anywhere anytime soon. Another trip probably won't hurt anything."

They walked back to the edge of the parachute, silently reached down for their sections, and threw their arms up. The colorful canvas billowed into the air above them.

## 21

Angela stood up, the solid ground beneath her feet holding her steady. The flooring was dark, something between muddy brown and purple, but hard to tell in the dim light. In front of her lay a vast emptiness, framing a dead silence with no breeze, and no source of light. The place simply *glowed* a pale green color like a bottle tossed by ocean tides and polished by sand.

Shawn yelled from somewhere in the space beyond what she could see, "Val!"

Angela sighed. It was probably hopeless, the chances of them finding Val, much less finding her alive. She glanced to her left at Jason.

He met her eyes with a half-smile. "We're gonna find her, Ang."

Shawn cried out again.

Angela was about to answer Jason, and was pondering a falsely hopeful response of, "Sure we will," versus what she really thought about all of it, when a scream in the distance cut through the haze.

"Shawn!"

Angela's eyes bulged and she spun around, searching for the voice. *Val's* voice.

Almost in unison, they all cried out, "Val!" and "Over here!" and "Where are you?!"

The pounding of feet echoed in the strange space and Shawn's voice drifted further away and... *down*, somehow, as he ran away from the parachute and toward the sound of Val's voice.

A small spark of hope bloomed in Angela's chest. Maybe Shawn could *see* Val. Could grab her and bring her back home. Then they could get Doug out of whatever he was caught in, fix Eric, and they could all leave. Go back to the beach house and play video games or fish or do whatever the hell they wanted to do. They could go *home*.

She stepped forward, testing the surface beneath her feet. It seemed solid enough. After a few more hesitant steps, she felt confident the ground would hold her and ran in the direction of Val's voice. She vaguely heard Jason yell, "Wait!" as the floor beneath her gave way and she fell.

She plunged downward through continuous layers of muddy brown and purple floors. Each space in-between was about ten feet high and tinted a different color. First, the green she had left behind, then a light blue almost as bright as the sky on a summer day. Next a deep red, dark and brooding, like the light that came from the red stained-glass windows in the old church. Then a blue green like the ocean just below the surface, but not so far down to lose the light.

Angela's scream echoed around her as she fell, and she could hear Jason to her left and slightly above her, yelling her name. He sounded as if he were also falling, his voice whisking between layers of the strange world they had found themselves in.

Warm air rushed by her as Angela continued her

descent, passing a yellow room so bright it seemed as if she were looking directly at the sun. She thought of her mom; yellow was her mom's favorite color. Angela wondered if she'd ever see her mother again, or her dad. She would do anything to see them again, she'd even eat that stupid casserole if it meant getting to go back home. She watched her tears float up and above her as she continued falling.

Angela passed through a pink room that had seriously strong vibes of a drunken night at Val's the previous summer when they had consumed so much watermelon Bacardi that they had thrown up. It was all Angela could do to convince her mom they had a stomach bug, and she should stay at Val's so she wouldn't "infect" anyone else.

A glimpse of green fabric fluttered out of the corner of Angela's eye as she dropped into a burnt orange room. The parachute. The green fabric edge of her section of the parachute peeked out from beneath the wall of each room she passed through. She didn't understand how it could work, and how she could be dropping through the exact same room so many times. Or, maybe there was an infinite number of that exact room? But maybe, if she could grab the edge of the fabric, it might be the *right* piece of the parachute.

She called out to Shawn and Jason, hoping someone would be able to hear her, "Try to grab onto your parachute but *don't lift it* until we all have it!" Angela screamed as she tried to push her way through the air toward the small, green flap. It was like dog paddling against a riptide. Just when it seemed impossible, Angela felt herself move an inch toward the fabric.

In the distance, she could hear Jason screaming down to her that he was good. Hopefully, Shawn was too. With one last grunt, Angela heaved herself toward the wall but could only graze the fabric with the tip of her fingers. As she fell through each room, and past each piece of the fabric, it fluttered against her fingertips, taunting her with the nearness and impossibility of her task. Angela bent forward and kicked her legs again.

She pinched the fabric with two fingers and lifted, hoping Shawn had heard her and made it back in time.

---

## 22

Angela stared across the limp parachute at the spot where Shawn *should* have been standing, and her heart sank. Nothing but emptiness hovered above the green cloth across from her. She glanced over at the place Eric had come to finally rest, just a few feet from the edge of the parachute between his spot and Shawn's. And then there was Doug, halfway to the broken window in the gym. Still semi-frozen in time. Still going for help.

Angela sobbed and fell to the floor. Jason rushed over and put his arms around her, squeezing tight. "It's gonna be ok. We're gonna fix all of this and everything will be back to normal."

She shoved him away, "You don't fucking *know* that! People don't come back from the *dead* Jason!" She pointed at Eric's body. "He's *dead*, can't you fucking see that? He's dead. Val is probably dead, Shawn didn't come back, and Doug ..." Angela choked back tears and shook her head, staring across the gym at Doug's back.

Jason stood and walked past Angela, toward Doug. She knew he was just trying to help, to make her feel better, but she knew they were stuck. They could try to go for help, but who's to say they wouldn't end up just like Doug? Or worse.

"It doesn't matter," Angela cried. "Nothing matters."

"Angela," Jason said from across the room, his voice quivering, "come here."

She looked up. Jason stood in front of Doug, staring at him with wide eyes. Angela jumped to her feet and ran. Once she came around to face her boyfriend, it felt like someone had punched her in the gut. She doubled over, hands on her stomach and bile in the back of her throat.

Doug was still alive, if she could call it that. He was still standing, still appeared to be breathing, but each small step forward seemed to take a thousand times longer than normal. She wasn't sure how much time had passed for Doug, but it was enough for him to grow a full beard, the ragged brown strands hanging down to his sunken chest. He had also lost weight. A *lot* of weight. His once-toned physique had dwindled to skin and bones. His clothes hung on his frame like they were three sizes too big. His cheeks were sunken in, and his eyes bulged from their sockets. Doug's mouth gaped slightly open, and his teeth looked larger, more pronounced as if his skin were shrinking and pulling back from them.

Knowing it wouldn't matter, but hoping anyway, Angela reached out to touch him.

Like before, her hands went straight through his chest.

"Jason," she whispered, "what's happening to him?"

"I don't know," he whispered back, staring at his friend.

Angela turned and ran back to the parachute. "Let's go. The sooner we get Shawn and Val back, the sooner we can figure all this out."

Jason didn't budge. "I'm going for help."

She swung around in shock. "What?"

"I'm going for help," he said and came closer. He reached out his hand, pulled her close to him, and kissed her. "In case I don't come back."

"No," Angela insisted. "NO. You are not going to leave me here with this..." she looked around the room.

"You know it makes sense, Angela."

"Who's to say it'll work? What if you get stuck like Doug?" she pleaded.

"Don't go under, then. Watch me."

"NO!" Tears welled up in her eyes, "you can't leave me, you're all I have now."

"Angela..."

"NO."

They stared at each other.

"I can't lose you," she whispered.

Jason sighed and took her in his arms. "Ok. Ok, I'm not going anywhere. We stick together."

They held hands and walked to the parachute. She stopped in front of the green fabric and Jason let go of her hand as he continued to the yellow fabric at her left.

They lifted the parachute.

## 23

Nothing happened.

She looked at Jason, confused.

"Maybe it's done?" Jason said. He turned to look at Doug. "Oh, shit."

"What?" Angela asked before turning to see for herself. "Oh god."

Doug was very much alive, still as thin as they had just seen, beard still just as long, but no longer frozen in time.

Doug sprinted across the gym, his footsteps pounding on the wooden floor. As soon as he got within arm's reach of the broken window, and the pounding footsteps turned into crunches over the broken glass, his whole body shimmered like he was standing in the middle of a hot road. Then he was gone, back at the edge of the parachute a few feet from Angela and Jason and running again.

"Doug!" Angela cried out, and his head swung around to face her, a look of terror on his face. He kept looking at her as he ran, stopped, shimmered, then reappeared close to her. She could barely see tears streaming down his face.

He couldn't stop.

Angela and Jason ran after him, but Doug had spent a few more years on the track team than either of them who, combined, had a total of zero experience running. They couldn't catch up. He was at the window and gone from view within seconds. They spun around to see him barreling toward them, eyes wide and mouth attempting to scream, but no sound came out.

He ran straight through them as if they weren't even there.

They spun around to see the back of him reach the other side of the gym, then disappear again. Before they could move, he exploded from their chests and kept running, passing through them without so much as a flutter.

Angela stepped aside, pulling Jason with her. She couldn't stand to watch him go through their bodies anymore. Couldn't stand to see this ghostly apparition of Doug. *Was* he a ghost? Was *she*? Were they stuck in that gym forever? Doug certainly *looked* alive, he even responded to her calling his name. But...

Jason grabbed Angela's hand and ran toward the parachute. She let him drag her, never taking her eyes off Doug as he continued to run, disappear, run...

Doug stared back at her, his dark brown eyes swimming in tears, until Jason lifted the edge of the parachute, and they were gone.

## 24

They were still in the gym, but Doug no longer sprinted toward the other end of the room. His body lay sprawled out on the wooden floor, just a few feet from the broken window.

Angela screamed.

They ran to Doug's side, but it was too late. He was gone. His dark brown skin, once healthy, now had a gray-blue tint to it. There were flaky pale patches scattered across his face and neck. His eyes were open, but the bright sparkling brown Angela had first noticed that day on the tennis courts had faded as if a haze had fallen over them. They stared straight ahead, and right through Angela.

She jerked away from him, bile rising in her throat. Angela hated herself for that reaction, for being disgusted by Doug. She should be falling over his body, screaming and crying like they did in the movies. But she didn't want to touch him. Didn't want to be in the same *room* with him. She ran to a corner of the gym, leaned her hands on her knees, and threw up.

When the last bit of bile had finally splattered to the

floor, Angela stood and wiped her mouth on her shirt sleeve. She would do anything for a bit of water at that moment, to wash down the remains of vomit in her mouth and ease the burning in her throat. She looked over at Doug's body, and a coldness shuddered through her skin. Jason was crouched, leaning over Doug and examining him for... what, exactly? He was clearly dead.

Angela walked back over to them but stopped a few feet away.

Jason looked up at her, tears in his eyes. "I can't believe this... I just... can't," Jason whispered. "It's a dream, that's all. Just a dream, and we'll wake up and this," he gestured at Doug, then at Eric's body, then the parachute, "will all be a distant memory."

"I think it's real," said Angela, as she stared down at Doug's body, her eyes avoiding his face. "It's fucking *insane*, but I don't think we're dreaming."

"We *have* to be dreaming. Otherwise, what the fuck is going on? This shit doesn't happen in real life. We don't live in a goddamn Wes Craven movie," said Jason, shaking his head and standing up.

"I have an idea," said Angela, bringing her eyes up to meet Jason's. "Maybe, if we get them back beneath the parachute..."

"We can undo it all?" Jason asked.

"Maybe," said Angela, though she knew it seemed more like a question.

They stared at Doug, then back at Eric.

Jason sighed, "Let's do it, then. What other options do we have?"

He slipped his arms beneath Doug's and linked his hands across his dead friend's chest. Jason glanced at Angela, started to say something, then stopped.

There was no way she would touch a dead body, be it Doug or anyone else.

Jason dragged Doug to the edge of the parachute next to Angela.

"Okay, you're going to *have* to touch him." Jason looked at her pointedly.

She avoided his stare. "I know."

Angela picked up Doug's still-warm hand and shivered. How long had he been dead? Had they just missed it happening? She shuddered thinking of having to watch him die. It was for the best, really, that he went before they came back. She hated herself for that selfish thought.

Jason moved next to Eric's body, picked up one of Eric's hands in his, and with the other, grabbed the green fabric. Shawn's section.

Jason and Angela looked at each other across the parachute. Before she could consider how far away they were, and if it would be worth it to move Eric's body closer, Jason lifted his arm.

Angela quickly followed, and the colorful fabric billowed above them.

## 25

Angela jerked her hand away from Doug's and wiped it on her shorts. What was she supposed to do? Like, be *happy* to touch a dead body?

At least it worked, and Doug had come through the parachute with her. She could only assume that Eric was with Jason across the... whatever.

Angela stood and looked around. She was in some sort of forest, filled with what looked like pine trees. They stretched above her for miles, fading off into the sky. The earth beneath her felt soft and damp. It smelled like the woods after a rain, earthy and pungent. There was a word for that, the way the earth smelled after a rainfall, but Angela could never remember what it was.

A strong wind blew in from her left, almost pushing her to the ground, then leaving as quickly as it had come. Somewhere off to her right, a bright chittering sound echoed in the distance. A few feet in front of her, leaves rustled as something came closer, the soft ground squelching with each step. She held her breath and ducked behind a tree with a glance at Doug's body laying out in the open. There wasn't anything she could do about him, bringing him back in hadn't helped anything. He was still very much dead.

The movements came closer, louder. A thick overgrowth of weeds near the base of a tree in front of her shifted and parted. Horns appeared, two identical light brown spirals jutting out from the bushes. At the top of each spiral, two shorter tapered tips pointed toward the sky.

Long, tan ears followed the horns, then a head like a deer, but the eyes were much larger than any deer Angela had ever seen. Her dad was a bowhunter, so she had seen her fair share of deer. She exhaled. Deer weren't anything to be afraid of.

The animal jerked and its ears twitched back and forth, listening while wide eyes searched the forest. Angela ducked her head behind the tree again, unsure if the deer had seen her. She moved around to the other side and peeked around the thick trunk. The deer's head leaned to one side, and it stepped forward from the brush, its eyes locked on Angela.

It was beautiful. Similar in body to the white-tail deer her father hunted, but with the strange eyes, spiraled horns, and overly large ears, there was no telling what the creature could be. Whatever it was or wasn't, it seemed friendly enough.

Walking toward Angela, it looked more curious than anything else. She relaxed and held out her hand. The deer stood inches from her when it suddenly stopped. The long ears pressed back against the narrow head and its large eyes widened even more. Before she could pull her hand away, the deer turned and bolted back into the bushes.

Branches broke in the distance, and a soft huffing noise permeated the space around her. Something was coming. Something bigger and faster than the deer.

Angela ran to the parachute, stepped over Doug's body, and lifted the edge of the fabric.

Nothing happened.

The small piece of cloth jutting out from beneath a tree flapped as she jerked it up and down. Tears streamed down her face as she pulled and yanked on the parachute's edge. Why wasn't anything happening? That was the rule, right? You lift the edge, you get to go back. She ran over the steps they had taken to get there, dragging Doug's body close to the parachute. She had held on to him while Jason held on to Eric.

*Jason.*

She had completely forgotten about him. Hoping his edge still worked, Angela ran in the direction she hoped he would be. If experience could be any indicator, she should be able to go straight ahead, and eventually she would come to him.

The crashing noises in the distance seemed to shift, running almost parallel with her. *Toward* Jason. Maybe he had already gone. Maybe he had already lifted his edge and that's why she couldn't. He wouldn't do that to her... would he? She shook her head as she ran, trying to ignore the fact that she had just done the same thing she was afraid of *him* doing.

Another strong gust of wind knocked her down. She jumped back up and continued running through the woods. The thing in the distance ran much faster, and as the broken branches and crunched leaves faded into the distance ahead of her, she heard Jason scream as she finally broke from the tree line and saw him.

He was holding a branch, waving it toward a massive creature in front of him, and screaming her name.

Of course, he wouldn't have lifted it without her. He loved her.

She would go to him, they'd lift the edge, and never return to that god-forsaken place. There was only one problem. That... *thing* stood between her and Jason, with its back to Angela.

She first thought it was an overgrown Chupacabra. It looked like a mangy coyote, thin and gaunt. But it was easily three times larger than any coyote she had ever seen. And larger than any pictures of Chupacabra she had seen in books.

Sharp spikes jutted out from tufts of matted hair along the creature's spine. As if a Stegosaurus and a Chupacabra had a baby. It stood up on two powerful hind legs, reaching out and swiping at the stick in Jason's hand.

The creature surged forward, knocked the branch away from Jason, and pounced on him with all four feet. Angela screamed, and the animal stopped and turned toward her. Its head seemed almost human-like, with a single eye taking up most of the face, bloodshot and with only a horizontal slit for a pupil. An eye staring straight at her.

She looked down at Jason. The skin had been completely removed from the right side of his face and his right arm. His shirt had been torn off and long, bloody scratches covered his chest. One was deep, and blood seemed to pour from it like a waterfall. Jason grimaced as his face paled, and his eyes fluttered. He had one hand on the edge of the parachute, but he didn't lift it. He wouldn't leave her, even as he faced death.

He made eye contact with Angela and yelled.

"Run!"

Angela couldn't move while the creature held her in its

gaze. It raised up again on two hind legs and took a step toward her.

"Hey!" Jason screamed, throwing a rock at the animal.

It ignored him.

"Hey!" He threw another rock, grunting from the effort.

It stopped and turned.

"Leave her alone—" Jason screamed as the animal pounced on him once again.

Amid the sounds of tearing flesh and bones snapping, as Jason's cry become a wet gurgle beneath the terrifying creature, Angela ran toward the parachute. She just needed to get to the edge...

The animal ripped into Jason's stomach, shoving his body against the edge of the parachute. Part of his arm went beneath it, and without sound or fanfare, both the parachute's edge and the upper half of Jason disappeared, leaving the creature's claws still holding onto his intestines and legs.

It seemed to have forgotten she stood there as it feasted on what was left of Jason, loudly smacking and cracking bones with its teeth.

Angela turned and ran.

## 26

The sun was high in the sky that bright October day as two men entered the Polk Elementary School gymnasium. They were both dressed in faded blue, long sleeved jumpers with patches reading "RPG Junk Removal" across their chest.

"Whoa, remember this?" One of the men asked as he spotted the parachute on the gym floor. He walked over and nudged it with the toe of his boot.

"Oh yeah," the other said softly, remembering better days. He smiled. "I call dibs."

"What? You can't call dibs, we're supposed to be junking this shit."

"Oh, come on, like you've never swiped something before? I saw that pit in the back of your truck last month."

The man laughed. "Hey it was practically like new, just needed legs. I didn't hear you complain when you were eating my brisket."

"Well, it's Kelly's birthday and I didn't get her anything yet. Was waitin' 'til payday." The other man crouched down next to the parachute and ran his fingertips along the edge of the canvas. "Think she'd like it? I'd prob'ly have to show her what to do— kids these days don't understand simple shit like this."

"How old is she gonna be?"

"Eight." He continued to stare at the colorful canvas in front of him.

"I *guarantee* you, she's not gonna want that old thing. I can spot you until payday, man. Get her somethin' nice."

The man stood up and adjusted the waist of his jumper. "You're probably right, but I'm taking it home anyway. Why waste a perfectly good parachute? Come on, help me roll it up."

They grunted as they leaned down and pushed the fabric into a tight sausage roll, then hoisted it onto their shoulders and carried it to their truck outside.


*THE END*

# ACKNOWLEDGMENTS

Thank you to Kennedy Mikel, Linda Hartsfield, Rebecca Rowland, Sue Cook, Charlie Rogers, Ryan Garcia, and Wayne Fenlon for reading an early copy and giving me valuable insights and tips to help make this book the best it could be. Thanks also to Wayne for designing the cover artwork, you truly captured the heart of this story. Thanks to NaNoWriMo, without which I wouldn't have had a (terrible, but complete) first draft. Thank you also to Erin Sweet Al-Mehairi for your edits!

To "The Rejects" Sara Dobbie, Rami Obeid, Megan Cannella, Travis Cravey, and Claire Taylor: Thank you for your support and friendship. 2021 was full of gut-punches, but we got through it.

Finally, thank you to the gang that used to night fish at the beach and hang out on the roof of the (not at all abandoned) elementary school.

# ABOUT THE AUTHOR

**Holly Rae Garcia** is the author of *Come Join the Murder* and *The Easton Falls Massacre: Bigfoot's Revenge*. Her short stories have appeared online and in print for various magazines and anthologies. She lives on the Texas Coast with her family and five large dogs. You can often find her reading, watching movies, or playing poker.

www.HollyRaeGarcia.com

# ALSO BY HOLLY RAE GARCIA

*The Easton Falls Massacre: Bigfoot's Revenge*

*Come Join the Murder*

Made in the USA
Columbia, SC
18 May 2022

60601976R00072